THE TRUTH ABOUT LOVE

"Hi, Zoe." Jeremy smiled. "I've got some-one I'd like you to meet."

Slowly, Zoe turned her head and found herself looking right into a pair of dark, dark brown eyes. They were the kind of eyes that made you melt. Zoe felt as if she were sinking down into their depths.

Ethan smiled. His teeth were white and perfectly straight. "Hi," he said. "I'm Ethan Anderson."

Returning his smile, Zoe wondered if this was what love at first sight was like, so easy, like falling from a great height in

Bantam Sweet Dreams Romances
Ask your bookseller for the books you have missed

THE TRUTH
ABOUT LOVE

Laurie Lykken

BANTAM BOOKS

NEW YORK • TORONTO • LONDON • SYDNEY • AUCKLAND

RL 6, age 11 and up

THE TRUTH ABOUT LOVE
A Bantam Book / March 1991

ISBN 0-553-28862-8

Published simultaneously in the United States and Canada

Bantam Books are published by Bantam Books, a division
of Bantam Doubleday Dell Publishing Group, Inc. Its trademark, consisting of the words "Bantam Books" and the
portrayal of a rooster, is Registered in U.S. Patent and
Trademark Office and in other countries. Marca Regis-
trada. Bantam Books, 666 Fifth Avenue, New York, New
York 10103.

PRINTED IN THE UNITED STATES OF AMERICA

OPM   0 9 8 7 6 5 4 3 2 1

For Morrie, who's missed

Chapter One

Zoe Reily put down her glass of orange juice and stared at her friend in disbelief. "Minda!" she exclaimed in an exasperated voice. "You know I'd do almost anything for you, but I can't do that!"

"Come on, Zoe. It's not for me, it's for Jeremy," Minda Davis coaxed.

Zoe sighed, and the other girls sitting at their table in the restaurant giggled.

Minda was a junior at Edenvale High, a class ahead of Zoe. Jeremy Brakken was Minda's boyfriend and the captain of the Edenvale swim team.

Zoe shook her head. "It doesn't matter. There's no way you're going to drag me to the

1

swim meet to fix me up with some strange guy." Privately, she wished that Jeremy had asked her for the favor himself. That way, she could have turned the whole thing into a flirtatious joke and Jeremy would have accepted defeat with a grin. Zoe knew that Minda didn't give up so easily.

"But you already promised to go to the swim meet with me tomorrow," Minda pointed out. She turned to the other members of the cheerleading squad at their table. There were six girls on the squad, counting Minda and Zoe: two each from the sophomore, junior, and senior classes at the high school.

"You all heard Zoe promise to go with me, didn't you?" Minda sounded just like she did when she was demanding a response from the fans at a game. Zoe half expected the four girls to shout out, "Yes!" at the top of their lungs.

But Marcy Wilkes, the other sophomore on the squad, came to Zoe's defense. "I heard Zoe say she'd go to the swim meet with you, Minda. But I never heard her *promise* anything."

"Look, Zoe," Minda began again, ignoring Marcy's comment, "think of it this way. Meeting this guy won't take any extra effort. You just have to smile and say hello, maybe shake his hand."

Zoe was about to retort that extra effort was hardly the point, but the waitress returned to the table with their breakfasts before she could.

Gathering at Merlin's Pancake House on the mornings before a game had become a ritual for the Edenvale cheerleading squad. It was a good way to get organized. They'd met this particular Friday morning in order to prepare for a boys' basketball game that night and a pep rally that afternoon. But their business had been taken care of quickly, and Minda had seized the opportunity to ask Zoe about letting Jeremy introduce her to one of his teammates at the swim meet.

The waitress gave Minda the first order of Merlin's Special Paper-Thin Pancakes. The next plate went to Kate Sholes, a senior and captain of the squad. The next order was Zoe's. As usual, the pancakes smelled delicious, and were the ideal food for a cold Minnesota morning.

Zoe had been very hungry when the girls had first arrived at Merlin's. But now the thought of being fixed up with some guy she'd never met started her stomach churning. She slowly started buttering her pancakes, trying to think of a graceful way to refuse. Zoe didn't want to do anything to jeopardize her friendship with Minda, but there were limits to what she was willing to do.

"Syrup?" Hanna Simms, a junior on the squad, offered Zoe a plate with a fat little glass pitcher on it.

Zoe took the plate. "Thanks, Hanna." She poured out the thick, golden syrup and watched it run down her stack of pancakes. *I don't have any trouble getting dates on my own*, she told herself. *I don't need to be fixed up, and I'm not interested in the kind of boy who needs to be*. She passed the pitcher to Minda.

"*Please*, Zoe," Minda said after finishing with the syrup herself. She fixed her bright blue eyes on Zoe, looking confident and hopeful at the same time. *It's now or never*, Zoe thought.

She took a deep breath, got set to refuse—and said, "I don't know." As soon as Zoe heard herself give that wishy-washy answer, she knew she'd lost the battle.

Minda knew it, too. She smiled radiantly. "It's not a real fix-up anyway," she assured Zoe. "It's just meeting him. You don't ever have to see him again after that if you don't want to. Jeremy says he's a great guy, though. He's sure you'll want to get to know him better after you've met him."

"Watch out, Zoe!" Marcy gave Zoe a sympathetic look as she shook her curly head. "When they tell you he's a great guy, it usually means he's a total loser."

Minda scowled at Marcy. "I wouldn't ask Zoe to meet just anyone. Besides, I've seen him, and he's a hunk. It's just that he's new in Edenvale, and it's tough to transfer during your junior year. It's hard to break into a group. Some kids don't even try."

"A hunk from our class, huh? What's his name?" Hanna asked as she sliced into her pancakes. She paused before popping the first bite into her mouth and added, "If I know him, I can tell Zoe whether you're telling the truth or not."

"His name is Ethan Anderson," Minda answered. "Do you know him?"

Hanna nodded excitedly, forcing herself to swallow. "Yes! He's in one of my classes. And you're right. Ethan's definitely a hunk, but he's really quiet. Maybe he's shy."

"What class do you have with him?" Zoe asked. She was beginning to feel a little interested in this mysterious boy despite her better judgment.

"English," Hanna replied. "Ethan hasn't said more than two words all year, and it's definitely not a quiet class."

"Even hunks can be shy," Kate offered sagely as she helped herself to more butter.

"I wonder if I've seen him around school," Zoe mused. She turned to Hanna. "What does he look like, anyway?"

"His hair is dark brown and kind of curly," Hanna said thoughtfully. "He's got really nice brown eyes, darker than yours even, almost black. They're big and sort of sad-looking— you know, the kind that make you melt. Oh yes, one more thing—he wears a red tie to school nearly every day," she added. "I'm not sure if it's the same one, but it always looks nice."

"I'm sorry, but he still sounds like a loser to me," Marcy said.

"I'm not fixing you up with him, Marcy," Minda said sweetly.

"I thought you weren't fixing me up with him, either," Zoe said. Minda smiled at her and shrugged.

"Ethan's not a loser," Hanna assured both Marcy and Zoe.

"I think you should do it," Kate said. "Go out with him, Zoe. Give the guy a break."

"At least meet him," Amy Bucklin, the

other senior, suggested. "Why not? It's not like you're seeing anyone regularly anyway."

"Okay, okay," Zoe said resentfully. She felt pressured by nearly everyone on the squad to give in to Minda. "I'll meet Ethan Anderson tomorrow, but that's all I'm going to do."

"That's all I was asking you to do," Minda said with a smile. "Thanks, Zoe! Jeremy will be happy."

"*Ethan* will be happy," Hanna predicted, smiling encouragingly at Zoe. "You two will make a terrific couple, I just know it."

"Hanna!" Zoe cried.

"Sorry," Hanna said, but she didn't look sorry at all.

"Can we drop this now and talk about something else?" Zoe pleaded. She was usually easygoing, but she was beginning to feel very cranky.

Minda shrugged. "Sure. What should we talk about?"

Once again, Marcy came to Zoe's rescue. "I heard that the senior boys are going to do another one of their awful skits right after Coach Polaski introduces the basketball team at the pep rally this afternoon," she remarked.

Minda groaned. "That means they'll dress up like cheerleaders again," she said. Then she grinned. "You know what would fix those guys? A taste of their own medicine. I think you ought to do a cartoon of them for the school paper, Zoe, one that makes them look really dumb. We'd get the last laugh and maybe they'd stop doing the same boring routine."

An image of the senior boys dressed like girls at the last pep rally of the football season flashed through Zoe's mind, and she laughed. "I could do that pretty easily," she agreed.

Zoe loved to draw and had had several of her cartoons published in the high school paper. This year she hadn't submitted any of her work, mostly because she'd been too busy with cheerleading. But before Zoe could get too excited, Kate dumped cold water on the idea.

"You could do it if you weren't a cheerleader, Zoe," Kate pointed out. "But we're representatives of our school's spirit, remember? We're not supposed to get involved in anything that would make trouble."

"I wouldn't do anything to make the squad look bad," Zoe assured Kate. "It would just be funny."

Kate looked as though she was about to say something else. But before she could, their waitress reappeared with the check. The girls quickly divided it among the six of them. Kate told Amy that it was her turn to leave the tip, which Amy did. Then the girls put on their coats and gathered up their things.

"Who's riding with me?" Kate asked, pausing by the glass doors to the parking lot. Both Kate and Hanna had driven that morning.

"Zoe and I should ride with Hanna," Minda said quickly. "You know, just in case she hasn't told us everything she knows about you-know-who."

Before Zoe could protest, Kate said, "Fine. Let's get going. Cheerleaders should never be late for school. It wouldn't look good."

"So," Minda said as soon as the three girls had gotten into Hanna's little red Toyota, "since you know Ethan Anderson from class and I don't, what else can you tell us, Hanna? Anything Zoe should know before tomorrow?"

"Minda!" Zoe cried. "Cut it out! I told you I'm going to meet this guy and I will. You don't have to keep trying to sell me on the idea."

"Forget it, Hanna. Zoe doesn't want to know anything else about Ethan," Minda

9

teased. "I guess she'd rather find out any of his deep, dark secrets on her own."

"I think that's always the best way," Hanna said with a straight face. She backed out of her parking space and followed Kate's green Ford out of Merlin's parking lot. "It's always more fun to be surprised."

Zoe threw up her hands in defeat. "Okay, I give up," she said. "Tell me everything you know about him, Hanna. Don't leave anything out. I want every gruesome detail."

Hanna cleared her throat. "Actually, I've already told you everything I know."

"Maybe we can get Zoe to sneak a peek at him today," Minda said thoughtfully. "When is your English class, Hanna? First period?"

Zoe emphatically shook her head. "No way. Forget it, Minda. I mean it. You got me to do this one thing, but that's it. I refuse to be humiliated."

"Okay, okay," Minda said. "No preview. Boy, you're touchy today, Zoe."

"Here we are," Hanna said. She pulled into the students' parking lot, parked the car, and turned off the engine. She was about to open the door when her mouth dropped open and she started giggling. "You're not going to believe this, but Ethan Anderson is right here. And he's heading this way!"

Zoe followed Hanna's gaze. A tall, broad-shouldered boy was walking toward them, wearing a red wool cap and a navy blue parka. It was impossible to tell whether or not he was wearing the tie Hanna had mentioned. But Zoe could see that he was dressed in khaki slacks and brown loafers that seemed conservative enough to go with a shirt and tie.

"That's Doug Anderson with him, isn't it, Hanna?" Minda asked. Hanna nodded. Zoe knew Doug, a senior, by sight from the Edenvale football team. She and the other girls had cheered him on all fall.

"Are Ethan and Doug related?" Zoe wondered aloud. Anderson was a common name, but it was possible. She watched the two boys joking and laughing as they walked past the car. Doug was huskier than long, lanky Ethan, but there was definitely a resemblance between them, especially around their dark eyes.

Hanna shook her head. "I don't think so. Ethan's new this year and I think Doug's lived here forever. I don't ever remember him mentioning Ethan."

"Ethan doesn't exactly look shy," Zoe commented.

"No, he doesn't," Hanna agreed. "Maybe he

just doesn't like our English class. He could be more interested in science and math."

"He's cute, though, isn't he?" Minda asked, giving Zoe a playful wink.

Zoe didn't answer. She thought Ethan Anderson was more than cute. He was handsome, so handsome that Zoe couldn't help wondering if he was a bit out of her league. She'd never dated anyone older than herself, either. Ethan was a junior, and that meant he was at least sixteen, maybe even seventeen, one or two years older than she.

"Go for it, Zoe," Hanna advised, as if she knew what Zoe was thinking. "I know I would if it weren't for Chuck." Hanna was dating Chuck Hollis, one of the basketball players.

"I would, too," Minda said thoughtfully, "if I weren't dating Jeremy, that is."

"He does look nice," Zoe admitted. "But he might not like me, so don't go making any long-range plans for us just yet."

"Of course he'll like you. Everyone likes you, Zoe," Minda insisted. "You're cute, fun, nice—"

"Okay, okay," Zoe said, cutting her off. "You're starting to embarrass me."

Suddenly the bell rang. The school grounds, which had been teeming with students just seconds earlier, were now nearly deserted. Almost everyone had gone in. Classes were about to start.

"Uh-oh!" Hanna exclaimed. "We're going to be late! And 'Cheerleaders do *not* get detention,' " she added, imitating Kate.

The three girls hurriedly left the car and started running across the field that separated the students' parking lot from the main building.

Once they were inside, the girls headed in three different directions. "See you at the pep rally," Minda called over her shoulder.

"Bye," Zoe responded. She took the gray marble stairs two at a time and dashed into her homeroom just as the tardy bell began to sound.

"Hi, Zoe," Jennifer Lund said as Zoe slipped breathlessly into the seat next to her. Their teacher wasn't in the room yet, and everyone was talking as loudly as if the bell had not rung.

"Hi, Jen," Zoe managed to say between gasps. Zoe and Jennifer had been best friends for a long time. They were close without having to do or even like the same things. And that was good because they were about as different as night and day. Jennifer's dream was to become a pediatrician. Zoe knew she

13

wanted to go to college but had no idea what she'd study. While Zoe was practicing cheers and yelling at games, Jennifer was either studying or volunteering at the local children's hospital.

"It'll help me get into a six-year med school program," Jennifer had explained when she'd first started spending nearly all her free time at the hospital. But Zoe knew that volunteering had become more than a college entrance requirement for her friend. Jennifer genuinely liked helping people at the hospital, and she was always trying to get Zoe to go with her. So far, Zoe had declined. Hospitals gave Zoe the creeps. Her beautiful young aunt Karen had died of cancer in one, and Zoe didn't want to go back inside another unless she absolutely had to.

"We're still going to go to the mall Sunday afternoon, right?" Zoe asked, once she'd caught her breath.

"Right," Jennifer agreed. "I'm working at the hospital Saturday, as usual. Want to come with me? The kids would love you."

Zoe shook her head. Jennifer would never give up trying to get her to go to the hospital, no matter how many times Zoe refused. In some ways, Minda and Jennifer were a lot alike, Zoe realized. Her two best friends were

14

stubborn and persistent. Both badgered Zoe to do things she didn't really want to do. Fortunately, she didn't find it as hard to say no to Jennifer, maybe because their friendship went back farther than Zoe's relatively recent friendship with Minda.

"I can't," Zoe said. "I just told Minda I'd go to the swim meet with her. She wants me to meet one of the guys on the team."

Jennifer raised her eyebrows. "Is she fixing you up with him?"

Zoe was quick to correct her. "I'm just going to meet him tomorrow, that's all."

"What's his name?" Jennifer asked. "Maybe I know him."

But before Zoe could tell Jennifer anything about him, Mrs. Wallace, their homeroom teacher, came rushing into the room.

"Sorry I'm late, class," Mrs. Wallace said breathlessly. "I had a little car trouble on my way to school." Jennifer raised her hand, and Mrs. Wallace nodded, giving her permission to speak.

"I've got the student-council minutes here, Mrs. Wallace," Jennifer said. "Can I read them now?"

"Please do," Mrs. Wallace said. Looking relieved, the frazzled teacher walked around her desk and collapsed into her chair. Jennifer got up, walked to the front of the room, and began to read the minutes aloud.

Zoe tried to pay attention to what Jennifer was saying about increasing the number of hall monitors and resolving problems in the lunchroom, but her mind kept drifting to the dark-haired boy she'd seen in the parking lot. She remembered the easy smile on Ethan's face. If he was only half as nice as he looked, he just might turn out to be someone she could really like.

Then Zoe shook her head. What was wrong with her? First she'd been upset with Minda for pressuring her into meeting a strange boy. Now she was daydreaming about that very same boy. If it had been May, or even April, Zoe could have blamed her confusion on spring fever. But it was only early December. She must be crazy. That was the only logical explanation.

Chapter Two

"What are your plans for today, sweetie? After you get your share of the housework done, that is," Mrs. Reily asked when Zoe drifted sleepily into the kitchen for something to eat on Saturday morning. The basketball team had won their game last night, and the cheerleaders, most of the basketball players, and a big group of other kids had gone out for pizza afterward. Zoe hadn't gotten home until a few minutes before midnight.

"Minda and I are going to the swim meet at school. She'll be picking me up later." Zoe yawned as she poured herself a glass of juice. She thought about telling her mother about

Ethan Anderson, but decided it was too soon to say anything about it. Besides, all she really knew about Ethan was that he was good-looking, and that hardly seemed enough to tell her mother.

Oddly enough, after never seeing him at all around school, Zoe had seen Ethan twice on Friday. She'd seen him before school in the parking lot, and she'd seen him again at the pep rally when Mr. Kinkakas, the swimming coach, had introduced the boys on the team. Ethan had seemed even better looking the second time Zoe saw him. The red tie he'd been wearing with his blue button-down shirt had really made him stand out among the other, more casually dressed guys. He'd also looked more mature than most of the boys he was sitting with, including Jeremy.

Zoe poured herself a bowl of cereal and carried it to the varnished maple table in the Reilys' cozy little breakfast nook, where her mother was sitting nursing a cup of thick black coffee.

"Maybe I should try some of that," Zoe said. "It might help me wake up."

"You're welcome to try it," her mother said with a wry smile. "But I don't think you're going to like it, at least not unless you add a lot of milk and sugar."

"I guess I'll skip it, then." Zoe doused her cereal with milk from the carton that had been left on the table, probably by Tara, Zoe's twelve-year-old sister. Tara was good at taking things out but terrible about putting them away again. "Scatterbrained" was the word their father used to describe her behavior. "What's Tara doing today, anyway?" Zoe asked.

"She and her friend Susan went to the mall. They said they wouldn't be back until late in the afternoon. What do you girls *do* at the mall, anyway?" her mother asked.

Zoe laughed. "Shop, of course. In fact, I'm going there tomorrow with Jennifer." They planned to do a little early shopping for the holidays, but Zoe didn't want to tell her mother that. Mrs. Reily, an attorney, was really busy at work these days, and Zoe didn't want her to feel pressured into doing a lot of gift shopping. Zoe's father had promised that he'd be home from his long business trip in Australia before Christmas, so there would be plenty of time for her parents to shop together then.

Sally Reily shook her head. "Shop, shop, shop. I never had time for that kind of thing when I was your age. I'm kind of surprised Jennifer does."

"Thanks a lot, Mom," Zoe said, pretending to sound offended. "You make it sound like you're not surprised *I* have time. I'm as busy as Jennifer is."

Mrs. Reily patted her older daughter's hand. "I know, honey. It's just that Jennifer has *serious* plans—I mean—"

"Give it up, Mom. You've put your foot so far into your mouth you'll never get it out," Zoe teased as she stood up. She picked up her empty cereal bowl and headed for the sink with it.

Mrs. Reily smiled ruefully. "I have, haven't I? Well, I'm sorry. I *am* glad you made the cheerleading squad," she said.

"But . . . ?"

"There are no buts. As your dad always says, 'Wouldn't it be boring if we were all alike?' "

"Absolutely." Zoe picked up her mother's cup and refilled it for her.

"Thanks, honey. You know I wouldn't trade you for anyone in the world," Mrs. Reily said fondly.

"I know." Zoe glanced at the kitchen clock. She had an hour and a half before Minda picked her up. "Guess I'd better get going on the vacuuming."

Mrs. Reily took another sip of her coffee,

then stood up too. "I'd better get to work myself. Is it my turn to dust?"

Zoe smiled. "You're bathrooms this week, Mom. Dusting goes with vacuuming."

"Ugh!" Mrs. Reily said. "No wonder I forgot. I hate bathrooms."

"We all do," Zoe assured her. "So don't bother asking me to trade. Besides, it's my turn next week. Maybe Tara will trade with you. It's her turn to do laundry and floor mopping."

"I'm afraid your sister is already finished with her chores. She did them last night while you were cheering at the basketball game. By the way, who won?"

"We did. It was really exciting. I wish you and Tara had come," Zoe said wistfully. "Our cheering was spectacular."

"I had that client dinner last night, remember?"

"Maybe I'll finally be able to get you to come out and watch me in action when Dad gets home," said Zoe. "I'd like that."

"I know, honey," her mother said softly.

"That's not a criticism, either," Zoe said quickly. "I know you're busy, and I understand."

"I know that, too. Now you better get going

or you won't be finished before your ride comes."

Once she'd gathered all her cleaning supplies, Zoe raced through her jobs. When she'd finished, she hurried upstairs to get ready for the swim meet. After changing her clothes, she sat down at her dressing table. First she brushed out her long reddish-brown hair until it shone. Then she added some mascara to darken her eyelashes and draw attention to her soft brown eyes. Finally, Zoe added a few strokes of blush to each cheek and a little clear gloss to her full lips. She smiled at her reflection to test the effect. Finally, satisfied with her appearance, she started downstairs to wait for Minda.

"I'm not going to tell them about it until you get home," Zoe heard her mother say as she passed the den. "This is something we really should tell them together, Will."

At the sound of her father's name, Zoe rushed into the den. "That's Dad, isn't it?" she demanded excitedly. "Can I talk to him?"

"It's Zoe, Will," Zoe's mother said. "She'd like to talk to you."

There was a little pause while her father was finishing whatever he'd been saying to her mother. Then Mrs. Reily handed Zoe the phone and quickly left the room.

"Dad! Where are you?" Zoe asked eagerly. She collapsed in the dilapidated leather chair that was her father's favorite when he was home.

"I'm still in Sydney. But I'll be on my way back in less than two weeks. Do you miss me?" he asked. His voice was so clear, it was hard to believe he was halfway around the world.

"You know I do!"

"How is everything?" Mr. Reily asked.

"Fantastic! This is the most perfect year of my life, or it will be once you get home. The basketball team is probably going to win the conference title and maybe even take state this year. The guys played Chester last night and won by thirty points. I'm going to go to the boys' swim meet today with Minda Davis. You don't know her yet, she's a junior and she's on the cheerleading squad with me. She's sort of my best friend. Of course, Jennifer's still my best friend too. But I think a person can have two best friends, don't you?" Zoe was so excited to be talking to her father that her words came rushing out.

Will Reily chuckled. "I don't see why not. People need all the friends they can get, best and otherwise. I'm glad you're having fun, honey." Then he added, "How's Tara? Is seventh grade treating her as well as tenth grade seems to be treating you?"

"I don't know," Zoe confessed. "We don't see each other very much. In fact, Tara was gone by the time I got up this morning. Mom said she was at the mall with one of her girl-friends."

Mr. Reily laughed. "All three of my girls seem to be busy—too busy to miss me very much."

"Not me!" Zoe declared firmly. "I'd never be too busy to miss you."

"But you are getting along all right without me?" It seemed like a strange question.

"I guess so," Zoe agreed halfheartedly. "But we'll all be glad when you come home."

"Is your mother still there? I need to finish talking to her," he said.

Zoe glanced over her shoulder and saw that her mother had come back. She was standing in the doorway, holding another cup of coffee.

"She's right here, Dad," Zoe said, waving her mother back to the phone.

"Good talking to you, honey," he said.

"Bye, Dad," Zoe said. Then she handed the phone back to her mother. As she left the room, Zoe thought she heard her mother say something about "rocking the boat." There was a funny edge to Mrs. Reily's voice that made Zoe pause for a moment in the doorway. But before she could hear any more of her mother's side of the conversation, Zoe heard Minda's car horn honk.

"I'm off," Zoe called. She pulled her ski parka out of the front hall closet and yanked open the door.

"Good-bye, honey," Zoe heard her mother call from the den. "Let me know if you're going to be late."

"I will," Zoe yelled as she bolted out the door. It was eleven-thirty on the nose. Minda was right on time.

Zoe slipped on her jacket as she hurried down the walk toward Minda's car, a vintage Mustang that really belonged to her older brother Stewart.

"Hi," Minda said as Zoe got in. She was looking at herself in the rearview mirror, patting her shoulder-length blond hair, which bounced and shimmered in the sunlight. Minda smiled at her reflection. Then she turned and smiled at Zoe. "I really like those black leggings," she said, nodding at Zoe's long legs. "What else are you wearing?"

"Just my rust-colored shirt. I thought it would be too hot by the pool for a sweater."

Minda raised her eyebrows. "Too hot by the

pool? Or too hot being so close to Ethan Anderson?"

"Don't start with me, Davis, or I just might change my mind about going through with this," Zoe said in a mock-threatening tone.

Minda laughed as she shifted the car into reverse. "You're not going to change your mind because I'm not going to let you. Jeremy's already told Ethan he's in for a spectacular surprise today. You don't want to disappoint him, do you?"

This time Zoe's frown was genuine. "Great," she grumbled, folding her arms across her chest. "What if he's disappointed after he meets me? Think how I'm going to feel!"

"He won't be disappointed," Minda insisted. "I don't know why you keep saying that, either. You're the prettiest girl in the sophomore class and one of the best-looking girls at Edenvale High. One of the nicest, too."

Zoe stole a quick look at herself in the rearview mirror when Minda stopped for a traffic light a few minutes later. She wondered if Minda was right. Zoe knew she was attractive, but was she really one of the prettiest girls in the school? She doubted it. Still, it was nice that her friend thought so highly of her.

The light turned green and Minda started

the car moving again. Zoe felt more uncomfortable the closer they got to the high school. She wished she knew more about Ethan Anderson. Maybe he wouldn't think she was so cute.

Who does he think he is, anyway? Zoe asked herself, suddenly angry. Boys shouldn't judge girls on their looks alone. Then she remembered that she'd judged him on *his* looks—that was all she had had to go by. What if he wasn't as nice as he was nice-looking? By the time Minda had parked the car next to the high school, Zoe felt totally frazzled.

"What's wrong?" Minda asked as the girls walked down the deserted hallway toward the observation area adjacent to the pool. "I don't think I've ever seen you so quiet. Do you feel okay?"

"No," Zoe said honestly.

Minda stopped walking. "Maybe I should take you home," she said worriedly.

"No way!" Zoe cried. There was no turning back now. "I'm going to go through with this if it kills me."

"Oh, I get it," Minda said, chuckling. "You're nervous about meeting Ethan, aren't you? I shouldn't be teasing you. Jeremy says he's really nice. I don't think he's terminally shy or anything, but I guess he is kind of shy around girls. Jeremy told me that he's been here since October and hasn't gone on a single date. Ethan wasn't even at that party Jeremy and I went to after the game last night."

"He wasn't?" Zoe asked. She wasn't sure whether this was good news or not.

Minda shook her head. "He was invited, but he didn't come. I think he needs you a lot more than you need him. That's what Jeremy seems to think, anyway. Like I said before, getting you two together was Jeremy's idea. He said he wanted to help Ethan learn to have some fun. Besides," she added, "Jeremy says a happy athlete is a better athlete, and he wants Ethan to be happy in Edenvale because he wants the guy to do his best for the swim team this season." Minda pulled open the doors to the observation deck, and they went in.

"There's Jeremy," Minda said as soon as the girls were sitting down. "Doesn't he look great?" Minda pointed at her slim, blond boyfriend, who was standing in the center of a cluster of other boys.

"Jeremy's a hunk, all right," Zoe agreed absently as she unsuccessfully scanned the pool deck for Ethan, whose dark good looks she found more appealing.

"Where's Ethan?" she whispered to Minda after a moment of fruitless searching.

Minda shrugged. "Don't worry. He'll be here. He's probably still in the locker room or something."

The Edenvale team was wearing gold racing briefs with a single white stripe on the right side. The word *Eagles* was written inside the white stripe in gold letters outlined in black. Mr. Kinkakas, the coach, was giving the boys a little pep talk. Zoe watched for a minute, but without Ethan there was nothing to hold her attention. Nervously she looked over at the other team.

The Richmond Tigers wore racing briefs in their school colors, orange and black. Gold and white, Zoe told herself, was much more heroic-looking. It gave the Edenvale team a clean-cut look. Zoe had a feeling that the Eagles were going to swim circles around the Tigers. But where was Ethan?

"I wish I'd thought to bring my sketch pad," Zoe said. Drawing had a calming effect on her and she definitely needed a little calming right now.

"Just don't put Jeremy in one of your cartoons," Minda warned. "He doesn't like to laugh at himself. He'd get mad."

Zoe nodded. "Some guys are like that," she

said. She wondered if Ethan Anderson took himself that seriously. She hoped he didn't. Zoe loved to laugh and she didn't like to have to hold back if she thought something was funny. Humor was a lot more fun if you could share it.

She looked back at the Edenvale team to see what poor, humorless Jeremy was up to. But instead of Jeremy, Zoe spotted Ethan. He was standing a little to the side of the rest of the team. He'd been handsome enough in his shirt, tie, and slacks. But in his gold-and-white racing briefs, Ethan Anderson looked as glamorous as a movie star!

Zoe poked Minda in the arm with her elbow. "There he is!" she muttered, nodding at Ethan.

"Good. Should I call them over?" Minda asked.

Zoe shook her head. "Not yet. Anyway, it looks like they're busy."

Just then Jeremy looked their way and waved. Minda waved back. Then Jeremy poked Ethan, and the two of them started walking around the edge of the pool toward the girls.

For a moment, Zoe couldn't breathe. "They're coming," she almost whispered to Minda.

"Relax." Minda giggled. "He's not going to bite you."

"Hey, Minda," Jeremy said casually. He leaned over the tile wall that separated the observation area from the pool deck, and Minda leaned toward him. Their lips met in a quick kiss. They separated, smiling dreamily at each other.

Then Jeremy seemed to remember they weren't alone. Turning to Zoe, he smiled and said, "Hi, Zoe. I've got someone I'd like you to meet."

Slowly, Zoe turned her head and found herself looking right into Ethan's dark, dark brown eyes. Hanna had said they were the kind of eyes that made you melt, and she was right. Zoe felt as if she were sinking down into their depths.

Ethan smiled. His teeth were white and perfectly straight. "Hi," he said. "I'm Ethan Anderson." As soon as he said his name, Zoe knew without a shadow of a doubt that he wasn't shy at all. He sounded much too poised. If he didn't talk much in English class, it was simply because there wasn't anything he cared to say.

"Hi," she said. As she returned his smile, she wondered if this was what love at first sight was like. It felt so easy, like falling from a great height in slow motion.

Ethan held out his hand. Zoe stared at it for a moment before realizing that he wanted to shake hands with her. His fingers, as they closed around hers, felt warm and dry. Ethan's smile widened as he gave her hand a gentle squeeze.

"I like your name," he said. His voice was deep and clear, warm and rich. "I looked it up. Zoe means 'life' in Greek."

Zoe nodded. She knew that, but the way Ethan said it gave it a whole new meaning for her. She silently thanked her father for choosing her name.

"If you two can stick around for a while after the meet, we'd like to take you out for pizza," Jeremy said. Zoe glanced at him in time to see him wink at Minda. *The two of them had this all planned!* she realized. She knew she ought to refuse—she'd already told Minda she was just going to meet Ethan today, not date him—but she couldn't do it. Because now, more than anything, she did want to go out with Ethan. She didn't really care where, she certainly wasn't hungry. At that moment, Zoe didn't think she'd ever be hungry again.

She looked back at Ethan and found that

he was still looking at her. "Pizza," he said, "or whatever you like, Zoe."

"Okay," Zoe said softly, aware that Ethan was still holding her hand.

"You guys better go back," Minda advised. "Mr. Kinkakas is sending a lot of anxious looks this way."

Jeremy glanced at their coach.

"Come on, Eth," he said to Ethan, then added to Minda and Zoe, "We'll see you guys after the meet, okay?"

"Absolutely," Minda agreed. She poked Zoe.

"Absolutely," Zoe parroted, watching Ethan as he followed Jeremy back to the other side of the pool.

"I don't think he's shy," Zoe said at last, struggling to catch her breath. "I guess Hanna was wrong about that."

"I guess so," Minda agreed. "And I don't think you have to worry about Ethan not liking you, either."

Zoe smiled. "I hope not, because I already like him—a lot!"

Chapter Three

"**W**asn't that fantastic?" Minda sighed. She and Zoe were outside the boys' locker room waiting for Jeremy and Ethan. The meet had ended fifteen minutes earlier, and the boys were still inside, showering and getting dressed.

Zoe nodded. "It really was exciting. You know, I wasn't sure what to expect before the meet started, but I loved it." She'd especially loved watching Ethan dive. He had looked so graceful as he sprang up, hovered in midair for a split second, and then slipped down into the water. But Zoe had enjoyed the other events as well, particularly the freestyle relay. Ethan had been in that event, too, and Zoe thought he swam as well as he dove.

Three of the other boys on the swim team came out of the locker room, said a quick hello to Minda and Zoe, and hurried off, talking eagerly about the team's first victory of the season.

At last Ethan came out, followed by Jeremy. Ethan's hair was still damp, and there were some wet little curls behind each of his ears. Zoe felt a sudden impulse to touch them.

"Hi," Ethan said. "Sorry we took so long. Some joker hid my socks."

Jeremy laughed. "That's what you get for those high scores of yours. Nothing below a six at the first meet isn't too shabby."

Ethan frowned and shook his head. "Not good enough, either."

Minda pointed at Ethan's feet. "Well," she said, "at least you found them."

"Not exactly," Ethan said, smiling. "These belong to the coach."

Just then, Coach Kinkakas came out of the locker room. Zoe looked down at his feet. He was wearing sneakers without socks. Zoe avoided looking at Minda, afraid that if she did, she'd giggle.

"Hello, ladies," the coach said. He nodded at Zoe and Minda, then turned to Ethan and Jeremy. "I'll see you guys Monday right after school. We're on a roll now and I want to keep that momentum going. We're going to work and practice hard." Looking down at Ethan's feet, he added, "Enjoy." Then he hurried off down the hall.

As soon as he was out of sight, all four of them burst out laughing.

"I like him." Ethan zipped up his jacket and pulled his red wool cap down over his ears. Then he looked down at his feet. "I like his socks, too."

"Where to?" Jeremy asked the girls.

"Zoe had pizza last night," Minda said. Zoe wanted to kick her friend for mentioning it, but Minda was out of reach.

"Okay. How about that taco place on Wilson Road?" Jeremy suggested.

"How does that sound, Zoe?" asked Ethan.

"That's fine with me. I love tacos," she said. "Actually, I wouldn't mind having pizza again, either. I love pizza too."

"You're easy to please," Ethan said matter-of-factly. Zoe gave him an inquiring look, and he laughed. "I'm taking mental notes," he explained. He closed his eyes for a minute and mumbled, "Nice eyes . . . loves tacos and pizza. . . ."

"Let's go," Jeremy said, tugging on the

sleeve of Ethan's jacket. "I'm starving. You can take your mental notes in the car."

When they got out to the parking lot, they decided that Jeremy and Minda would take Minda's car and Zoe would ride with Ethan. They'd meet at Taco John's.

"So," Zoe began once the two of them were alone in Ethan's car, "you're new to Edenvale, right?"

Ethan smiled. "Yes and no. My dad grew up here and came back with my mother after they finished college. I was born right here in North Memorial Hospital." He started the car and followed Jeremy, who was driving Minda's brother's car out of the lot.

"Really? So was I!" Zoe exclaimed. Then she laughed because she'd sounded so excited. "That's a dumb thing to get all worked up about, isn't it?"

Ethan shook his head. "I don't think so. It's one more thing we have in common, like liking pizza and tacos. That's important stuff to keep track of when you're just getting to know someone."

"It is, huh?" Zoe teased.

"Of course it is."

The light at the corner turned red just as Ethan reached the intersection. Jeremy had made it through, though, and kept driving.

"I hope you know where the taco place is, because I don't," Ethan said as a car pulled out of a driveway, blocking the Mustang from their sight.

Zoe smiled. "Yes, I do. Anyway, I interrupted your story."

"Was I telling a story?" he asked. The light turned green again.

Zoe nodded. "Yes. You were telling me the story of your life. So tell me more."

"I was? Well, let's see then. I was born here, but my parents moved to Arizona a couple years later."

"Arizona?" Zoe asked. She didn't mean to keep interrupting, but Arizona was one of the places she'd always wanted to visit.

Ethan grinned. "It's a pretty amazing place, actually."

"I'd love to live someplace that was warm all the time like that," Zoe told him.

"Sorry to have to disappoint you, but it isn't warm all the time."

"It's got to be warmer than it is here."

"That's true enough," Ethan agreed.

"Turn left at the next corner," Zoe instructed him. After Ethan made the turn, she went on, "Weren't you upset at having to leave Arizona?"

"No, it was my choice. Actually, my family

is still there. I'm living with my aunt and uncle. Do you know my cousin Doug?"

"Doug Anderson!" Zoe exclaimed. She turned in her seat and looked at Ethan's profile. She'd been right after all. There *was* a family resemblance between the two boys. She felt the way she used to when she'd find one of the pieces of her father's jigsaw puzzles for him.

"Do you know Doug?" Ethan asked.

"Just from the football team, you know, from cheering at the games," Zoe explained. "I'm just a sophomore. Doug's a senior." She felt embarrassed. "But of course you know that." Out of the corner of her eye she saw Taco John's. They were driving right by it.

"Uh-oh," she said. "We just passed the restaurant. So much for my great navigational skills."

Ethan chuckled. "No problem. I can turn around at the gas station up there on the corner."

"We thought you'd decided to go somewhere else," Minda teased when Zoe and Ethan joined her and Jeremy at the entrance to the restaurant.

Zoe couldn't help blushing. "That was my fault. I forgot to pay attention."

"You lost us back at that light," Ethan

said, giving Jeremy a playful punch on the arm. "You make a lousy guide. Remind me never to go mountain climbing with you. You'd probably go right over the top and leave me stranded on the other side in an incredible blizzard!"

"Sorry," Jeremy apologized sheepishly. "This one was distracting me." He put his arm around Minda and pulled her close. Minda giggled as she playfully pushed him away.

Ethan opened the restaurant door and held it for the others. "Let's go in. I'm freezing."

"Not used to Minnesota winters yet, huh?" Jeremy observed as he followed Minda inside.

"Not yet," Ethan admitted.

"You're in big trouble," Jeremy warned. "It's not really winter yet, you know. It won't be until the twenty-first. Then wait until January! Sixty-below-zero windchills are the norm. Your hair will freeze after meets. Mine always does."

All four of them sat down at a table, and Ethan pretended to shudder. "Maybe I'll invest in some electric socks—that is, unless the coach already has some I can borrow."

As the boys continued talking, Zoe took a pencil out of her purse and quickly sketched

Ethan on the white paper place mat. In her drawing, he was completely bundled up in heavy clothes, with wires coming down from his electric hat and up from his electric socks. She added electric mittens with wires running up his arms.

"Look at this, you guys," Minda cried, snatching Zoe's place mat and holding it up so the boys could see. "Zoe strikes again!"

"Hey, that's me!" Zoe was glad to hear Ethan laugh when he recognized himself. He grinned at her. "You're good."

Zoe smiled shyly. "Thanks."

"Just don't do me," Jeremy said, covering his face with his hands.

"Don't worry, I've already warned her about you," Minda said. Jeremy wadded up his napkin and tossed it in Minda's direction.

"Can I keep it?" Ethan asked Zoe.

"Sure," Zoe said. She watched him carefully fold the place mat and tuck it into a zippered pocket of his jacket.

A waitress appeared and handed out menus.

"I love Mexican food," Minda said with a happy sigh.

"Is this authentic Mexican?" Ethan asked, lifting one dark eyebrow.

"Just to show you that I take your question

41

seriously, we'll order two of their big combination dinners and four plates," Jeremy said. "That way, you can see for yourself."

"You mean *taste* for yourself, don't you?" Zoe said. Everyone laughed, and Zoe realized she was feeling more and more relaxed by the minute. Ethan was as easy to be with as he was to look at, she told herself happily.

When the waitress came back with the pitcher of root beer Ethan had asked for, Jeremy ordered. Then the boys started talking about the meet.

"I'm going to the bathroom," Minda whispered to Zoe. "Come with me?" Zoe nodded, and they slipped away.

"Well?" Minda demanded as soon as the girls were standing in front of the long mirror.

"Well, what?" Zoe countered, although she knew perfectly well that Minda wanted to know what she thought of Ethan. Zoe took her brush out of her purse and began running it slowly through her long hair.

"How was the car ride? What was it like being alone with him?" Minda demanded eagerly. She'd gotten out her comb but she wasn't using it.

Zoe grinned wickedly. "He's very nice," she said as she put her hairbrush away.

"Nice!" Minda exclaimed in an exasperated voice. Zoe could tell Minda was getting ready to accuse her of making the understatement of the year, when two middle-aged women came into the rest room and joined them at the mirror. Minda didn't say anything. Zoe put on a little fresh lip gloss.

Minda shook her head. "Come on, you," she said. She took hold of the sleeve of Zoe's blouse and pulled her toward the door. "You look great and you know it."

When they got back to the table, they found that the food had arrived and the boys were already eating.

"How is it?" Zoe asked Ethan as she sat back down. "As good as you can get in Arizona?"

Ethan shrugged. "It's not as spicy, but it's good. What would you like?"

Zoe pointed to a cheese enchilada. "That."

"Give me your fork," he ordered. He skillfully scooped it onto Zoe's plate and added some rice and beans.

Ethan told them a little bit about his high school in Arizona while they ate. But he didn't mention his reason for coming to Minnesota, and Zoe was becoming very curious. Why would a championship diver leave a place that seemed to be ideal for his sport?

It might be because of something he didn't want to talk about. Maybe his parents had split up. In any case, it was clear he wasn't eager to discuss it.

"Where to now?" Jeremy asked when all the food was gone. He leaned back in his chair and patted his stomach contentedly.

Without looking over at Zoe, Ethan said, "I have to get home, I'm afraid."

"Me, too," Zoe said quickly.

"What a couple of party poopers," Jeremy declared. "Minda and I are going to a movie later. Why don't you guys come along?"

This time Ethan did glance over at Zoe. "Another time?" he asked her. Zoe nodded.

As they were getting ready to leave, Minda pulled Zoe aside. "Ethan really likes you," she whispered. "I can tell."

Zoe was about to say that she really liked him, too, but then there he was, casually draping his arm across Zoe's shoulders. The gesture gave her goose bumps all over her arms. She was glad she was wearing a jacket so the others couldn't see the effect Ethan had on her.

"See you later," he told Jeremy and Minda. He and Zoe walked out to his car.

"You'll have to give me directions again," he said as he stopped the car at the end of the driveway leading out of the restaurant's parking lot.

"I hope I do a better job this time. I kind of spaced out on you before," she said apologetically.

"Oh, I don't know," Ethan mused. "You did all right. I mean, we got where we were going, didn't we?"

"True. Turn right here," she said when they reached the stop light.

"What street do you live on?" he asked.

"Colfax."

"And the streets in Edenvale are in alphabetical order, right?" Zoe nodded. "This is Arden. The next street is Beard. And that means that the next once is . . ."

"Colfax," Zoe finished for him.

But instead of turning and going up the two blocks to Colfax, Ethan pulled over to the curb and stopped.

Zoe looked at him curiously. "I don't live here," she said.

"I know. I just wanted to talk a little more before we got to your house. I wish we could go out tonight, but I promised my cousin I'd do something with him," Ethan said.

"You don't have to explain."

"I know, but I wanted to. Will you go out with me some other time?" he asked.

Zoe smiled and nodded. "I'd like that."

"How about next Friday?"

Zoe frowned. "I'm cheering next Friday at the basketball game." For the first time since making the squad the spring of her freshman year, she almost regretted her cheerleading commitment.

"What about after the game?" Ethan asked.

"Okay," Zoe agreed. "Maybe we can double with Jeremy and Minda again."

"Good idea," he said. Then he leaned over and gave Zoe a quick kiss on the tip of her nose. "I'm real glad I met you, Zoe." He patted his jacket pocket. "I'm going to send this drawing to my mother. She'll love it." With that, he put the car in gear again and took Zoe the rest of the way home.

A few minutes later, Zoe was letting herself into the house. As soon as she was inside, she touched the tip of her nose. It still felt warm from Ethan's kiss.

She felt she had to tell someone about meeting Ethan. It was so exciting, she couldn't keep all her feelings inside. But Mrs. Reily was out, and Tara wasn't home either, so Zoe dashed into the den to call Jennifer.

"Sorry, Zoe," Mrs. Lund said when she

answered the phone. "Jennifer's still at the hospital."

Of course, Zoe thought. *Jennifer's always at the hospital. How could I have forgotten?* "When do you think she will be home, Mrs. Lund?"

"I'm not sure. She's working on that big holiday party today. It's quite a project, you know."

Zoe certainly did know. Jennifer had been pestering her to help with it for the last couple of weeks.

"Shall I have her call you when she gets home, Zoe?" Mrs. Lund asked.

"Thanks," Zoe replied. "That would be great."

As soon as she hung up, Zoe dashed upstairs and got out her sketch pad. She drew Ethan in his swimsuit, Ethan in his ski jacket, Ethan smiling, Ethan looking pensive. She'd filled several pages with drawings of him when the phone rang. Springing off the pale blue comforter that covered her bed, Zoe dashed into the hall to answer it.

"Well?" Jennifer said as soon as Zoe picked up. "How did the big meet go?"

"We won," Zoe said dreamily.

"I'm not talking about the *swim* meet, you dope," Jennifer said. Zoe could almost see her friend shake her head at Zoe's denseness. "I'm talking about the big meet between you and Jeremy Brakken's friend."

Zoe laughed. "I think we won that, too. We're going out next Friday night!"

"Hmm," Jennifer said thoughtfully. "Sounds like the boy moves fast—in more ways than one."

Even though Jennifer couldn't see her, Zoe nodded. Then she sighed. "Oh, Jen, I think I'm in love!"

Chapter Four

"You don't *look* different," Jennifer said when Zoe met her Sunday afternoon in front of Juniors! Juniors!, a trendy clothing store in the Edenvale mall.

"What do you mean?"

Jennifer smiled as she tucked a wisp of her straight dark blond hair behind her ear. "I thought you were supposed to look different after you fell in love."

"Who said anything about falling in love?" Zoe said, but she was smiling. Just thinking about Ethan gave her goose bumps. If that wasn't love, she asked herself, what was?

"You did, remember? Yesterday afternoon? On the telephone?" Jennifer prompted. "In fact, you practically talked my ear off yesterday."

Zoe sighed and shook her head. "I shouldn't have said so much."

Jennifer grinned. "What are best friends for? Anyway, your secret, if it still *is* a secret, is safe with me. You know that. Now, where are we going to go first?"

Zoe pulled out her gift list. It was a little early to be shopping for Christmas presents, but Zoe and Jennifer had discovered a long time ago that shopping early was best. Zoe scanned the names on her list for a minute, then tucked it back into her brown leather shoulder bag. "I don't know where to start," she said. "I guess I'm a little scatterbrained today."

"How about starting with Ethan's gift?" Jennifer suggested mischievously.

"Ethan isn't on my list. I just met him yesterday," Zoe reminded her.

"You don't have to actually buy anything for him. We can just window-shop," Jennifer suggested. "That way, if you decide at the last minute that you want to give him something, you can run right out and pick it up."

"I don't think we should waste the time," Zoe said, but her mind was already spinning with possibilities. She could get Ethan a pair of wild-looking socks. Or she could get him a tie, like the skinny red one she'd seen him wearing at school on Friday. But she'd get him one in a different color, maybe an electric blue. Ethan would look great in electric blue, she told herself. Or she could draw him another picture. He really had seemed to like the silly, quick sketch she'd done. She could do another one that Ethan could keep for himself. She'd even get it framed for him.

"Let's start with our mothers, then," Jennifer said, obviously unaware of how her suggestion had affected Zoe. "Mine wants an electric wok. I'm not sure I can afford that, though. What does your mother want?"

Zoe didn't have to look at her list to answer that. "She wants Dad to come home. You wouldn't believe how grouchy Mom's been lately. A three-month business trip is too long. I thought so before Dad left, and now I know so."

"I think your mother's been a good sport about the whole thing. My mom would hit the ceiling if my dad said he was going to go to Australia for so long, and my mom only has a part-time volunteer job at the art center to deal with, not a legal career," Jennifer said.

"That and three more kids than my mother

has. Mom wasn't happy about it. There just wasn't anything she could do to stop him." Zoe started toward Alsted's Department Store, and Jennifer fell in step. "Anyway, I decided to get her a new nightgown for Christmas. The ones she has are practically rags, and she's just too busy to shop for one for herself."

"That's a great idea! We'll look in the lingerie department first. Then we'll go up to housewares," Jennifer said in her take-charge voice. She started walking faster and reached the door to Alsted's first. The girls proceeded to lingerie and browsed in the nightgown section.

"How about this one?" Jennifer asked. She had pulled a bright red lace nightgown off the rack. She held it up to her slim frame and batted her eyelashes at Zoe. Zoe laughed. Though Jennifer was pretty, with dark blond hair and moss-green eyes, she wasn't the eyelash-batting type.

"My mom's more the flannel-nightgown type," Zoe said.

"Ugh!" Jennifer exclaimed. "I thought this was for your dad's homecoming."

"Maybe a little," Zoe admitted. "But it's mostly for Christmas. Mom definitely wouldn't wear that. She'd say thank you and then tuck it away. And if I asked about it, she'd smile and tell me it was too pretty to wear."

"How about this?" Jennifer asked, holding up the same style as the red one, only in black.

"Flannel," Zoe insisted. "I think Dad likes flannel, too." Zoe smiled fondly as she thought of her father. "He'd think flannel was cozy."

Jennifer shook her head in mock disgust. "A *wok* is a hotter present than a flannel nightgown! Maybe you should wait and feel your mother out about this," she suggested. "Let's head for housewares."

A few minutes later, Jennifer was closely examining the electric wok the sales clerk had taken out of its box. She turned to Zoe. "What do you think?"

"If it's what your mother wants, go for it," Zoe advised. "I think you're lucky to find it on sale."

"It won't be on sale next week," the saleswoman agreed eagerly, patting the red lid of the wok. "We might even sell out of them at this price. These things make an ideal gift. I've sold three already today."

"All right," Jennifer said. "I'm sold." She opened her bag and took out her wallet.

As she and Zoe waited for the clerk to ring up the sale, Zoe heard a familiar male voice calling her name. She spun around, not quite believing it was Ethan, but it was. She waved and he came over to them.

"Hi, Ethan," Zoe said, blushing. She nodded at Jennifer. "This is my friend Jennifer Lund. Jennifer, this is Ethan Anderson."

Jennifer smiled. "Nice to meet you," she said.

"Here you go," the saleswoman said, interrupting them, and reaching over the counter with a large shopping bag.

"Ugh," Jennifer said as she took it. "I didn't think about having to carry this around the rest of the time while we shop. It's not heavy, but it's kind of bulky."

"What is it?" Ethan asked.

"A wok. For my mother," Jennifer explained.

"We're doing a little early holiday shopping," Zoe supplied.

Ethan grinned. "That's exactly what I'm doing. I have to get stuff wrapped and in the mail to Arizona this week or it won't get there in time." He looked at the display of woks. "Both my mom and dad might like that. One of their favorite things to do is cook together."

"An excellent choice," the saleswoman said.

"They won't be on sale after this week," Jennifer added.

"Meanwhile," Zoe put in, trying not to giggle, "they might sell out."

"Sold!" Ethan cried. "I'll take it."

As the saleswoman hurried off with Ethan's money, Zoe decided that she'd been wrong about Ethan's family. If Ethan was buying a wok for both of his parents, they couldn't have split up. There had to be some other reason why he had left his family. But what was it?

"I think we should get a piece of that clerk's commission," Jennifer joked. "We made her job way too easy for her!"

"I've got a better idea," Ethan said. "How about letting me buy you Cokes or something? It's the least I can do. I'd have been stewing over what to get for hours if I hadn't run into you like this."

"Sounds good to me," Jennifer said, glancing at Zoe. "I know I could use a break." They hadn't even been at the mall an hour yet, so Zoe knew Jennifer was just doing this for her.

As soon as Ethan got his wok, the three of them took the escalator back down to the main floor. When they reached the door that led from Alsted's to the center court of the mall, Ethan said, "You'll have to tell me where to go. I'm new in town, remember."

"Definitely the food pit," Jennifer said.

Zoe nodded. "Definitely."

Ethan's dark eyebrows shot up, and he made a face. "The *food pit*?" He opened the door and held it for the girls.

"I know, I know," Jennifer said, leading the way. "It sounds awful, and it is. Still, it's the best place for a quick Coke." They walked over to the railing and all three of them looked down.

"There it is," Zoe told Ethan. "That's the food pit. At least, that's what we call it."

"The mall is a little grander about it," Jennifer said. "They call it the centralized refreshment area."

Zoe laughed. "You just made that up."

Jennifer shrugged. "True. But it does sound like a name the mall would come up with, doesn't it?"

Ethan was laughing now, too. "It sure does," he agreed. Then he put an arm across Zoe's shoulders. "Let's go!"

While Ethan went to one of the counters to buy their sodas, Jennifer and Zoe found an empty table and sat down.

"So, what do you think?" Zoe asked eagerly when the two girls were alone.

"About what?"

"About Ethan, of course," Zoe said, even though she knew Jennifer was teasing her.

"I think it's a good thing you met him," Jennifer said. "A good thing for you, that is. He's a doll."

"He *is* nice," Zoe agreed.

"And good-looking," Jennifer nodded.

"And athletic," Zoe went on.

"And almost over here," Jennifer remarked. "We'd better talk about something else."

Ethan returned to their table just seconds later, handed them their Cokes, and then sat down.

"So," Zoe said, after she'd thanked him for the Coke, "how was the hospital yesterday, Jennifer?"

"What hospital?" Ethan asked.

"Jennifer volunteers at Children's Hospital," Zoe explained.

Jennifer's eyes lit up as she started on her favorite topic. "Right now we're planning a holiday party. It's officially a winter-solstice party so we don't offend anyone who's religious. The kids are all in on the planning. There's even one little guy who's disappointed because he's gotten well enough to go home before the party."

"Can't he come back?" Zoe asked.

Jennifer nodded. "Sure. That's what we told him."

"Once he gets home, he might not want to come back," Ethan said. He sounded so serious that both Jennifer and Zoe gave him questioning looks. When he noticed their expressions, he smiled and shrugged. "Just a thought," he said.

"I've got a terrific idea," Jennifer said. "Why don't you guys come to the party? Having a diving star and a cheerleader there would really inspire some of the kids!"

Zoe couldn't believe it. Jennifer was pushing the hospital again! Zoe looked quickly over at Ethan. Ordinarily, she would just refuse and that would be it. Zoe didn't want Ethan to think she was the kind of girl who didn't help other people, but he seemed as uncomfortable with Jennifer's suggestion as she was.

"When is this party?" Ethan hedged, frowning slightly as he wiggled his straw back and forth in his Coke.

"December twenty-first," Jennifer said. "That's the first Monday of our vacation." Realizing that she was putting Ethan on the spot, she backed down a little. "You can let me know, Ethan. I mean, you don't have to tell me today. I know the kids would like it, though. And the more help we have when we do something big like this, the better."

Ethan nodded thoughtfully and his expression softened. "I'll definitely think about it and let you know, okay?"

"Maybe we should go back to our shopping," Zoe said. "My mom's picking me up in an hour, and I haven't found a single present yet."

"And I've got to find my cousin Doug," Ethan said, rising from the table. "Maybe you can tell me how to get to Birchman's."

The girls looked at each other, confused. "Do you mean the florist's?" Zoe asked.

Ethan nodded. "Isn't it called Birchman's?"

"It probably should be," Jennifer said. "Birchman's sounds like a place that sells plants. But it's Berman's. I think that's a family name."

"Why don't you and Jennifer show me the way?" he asked Zoe. "That way I won't get lost."

When they got to the florist's, they found Doug Anderson sitting on a bench out front.

"About time," he said, standing up. "I was about to send out a search party."

"No need for that. I ran into Zoe," Ethan

said. He looked at Zoe and smiled. Then he added, "And this is Zoe's friend Jennifer."

Doug grinned at Jennifer. "I've seen you before at school."

"Probably," Jennifer agreed. "I'm there five days a week. Well, guys, I have to get going. I have to go to Music City," she said. "My brother's getting a CD player from our parents, and the rest of us are getting him discs for it."

"That's a good idea. Maybe I'll get a new tape for Tara," Zoe said.

"Is that your sister?" asked Ethan. When Zoe nodded, he said, "How old is she?"

"Twelve," Zoe replied, wrinkling up her nose. "It's kind of a difficult age."

"My sister's twelve, too," Ethan said. "That's one more thing we have in common."

"They're piling up fast," Zoe said.

"Speaking of fast, we better move fast or we're going to run out of shopping time," Jennifer warned.

"Sounds like we're about to go our separate ways," Ethan said. Zoe thought he sounded a little wistful about it. "I'll call you tonight," he told her. "Nice meeting you, Jennifer."

"Yeah," Doug added. He and Ethan went into the florist's while Jennifer and Zoe headed across the courtyard to the wing where Music City was located.

As the girls were looking over the bins of CDs and cassettes, Jennifer said, "I hope you and Ethan will come to the party. I meant it when I said the kids would get a kick out of having you there. And the rest of us would be thrilled to have your help."

"I don't think Ethan was too excited about the idea," Zoe said, remembering the look that had come over his face when Jennifer suggested it.

"I think he was just waiting to find out what you thought about it," Jennifer said. She moved from the *J* bin to the *K* bin and Zoe followed her.

"Well, you know what I think about it. Hospitals give me the creeps. They make me think of death," Zoe said, shivering slightly.

Jennifer looked up from the bin and shook her head. "You've got to get over that. Most of the people who go into hospitals come back out again feeling a lot better, and many of them are even cured."

"And some die in there," Zoe insisted. "My aunt did."

Jennifer moved to the *L* bin. "I know, and I'm sorry."

Zoe nodded. She was remembering how

her aunt had been a little sicker each time they'd gone to see her, and the memory made her feel sad. "Let's talk about something else," she said. She pulled a Love And Rockets tape out of the *L* bin and showed it to Jennifer. "Do you think listening to this would snap my grouchy little sister out of her preteen funk?"

Jennifer laughed. "Either that or throw her farther into it. I don't think there's any middle ground with kids that age. Maybe you should get her a Debbie Gibson tape instead."

Zoe put the tape back in the bin. "You're right," she said.

Jennifer suddenly looked serious. "Listen, Zoe. I don't want to push you too hard. But promise you'll think about the hospital thing some more. Helping out would be good for you."

Zoe sighed. "I'll think about it, okay? But only if you'll drop it for now."

Jennifer smiled at her. "Consider it dropped."

Chapter Five

"Let's go sit with Jeremy and Ethan during halftime," Minda suggested to Zoe as the girls came running off the basketball court Friday night. The Edenvale Eagles were leading by ten points with just a few seconds of the first half to go. The Wildon Warriors had just had a time-out to regroup their offensive strategy, and Zoe and the other Edenvale cheerleaders had taken the opportunity to get the Eagles' fans cheering.

"Do you know where they're sitting?" Zoe asked. She quickly scanned the bleachers on the Edenvale side of the court, but didn't see them.

"They were up there last time I saw them."

Minda nodded at the top of the middle section.

Zoe turned around and looked where Minda was looking.

"See them?" Minda asked.

Zoe scanned the crowd. Eventually, she spotted Ethan. He wasn't sitting right next to Jeremy, but they were in the same section. Ethan seemed to be the only person up there who wasn't a senior.

Zoe hadn't really seen Ethan since they'd met at the mall. She'd spoken to him a couple of times on the telephone, but they seemed to be on completely different schedules at school. They didn't even have the same lunch period.

"I see them now," Zoe said. Her cheeks felt warm.

"Want to go up at the half, then?" Minda asked.

"Sure. Maybe we can get Ethan to tell us where we're going after the game," Zoe said. "You don't know, do you? Does Jeremy?"

"I don't think so," Minda replied. "This is all Ethan's plan."

"That's kind of surprising, isn't it? I mean, last week he didn't even know where Taco John's was," Zoe commented just as one of the Warriors sank a three-point basket.

Minda groaned. The other cheerleaders started chanting, "Hold them back! Hold them back! *Way . . . back!*" and Zoe and Minda joined in.

When the Eagles threw in the ball it was stolen by the Warriors' center. The center passed the ball to the forward but before he could get any farther down the court, their coach signaled for a time-out. As soon as the players had run off the court, Zoe, Minda, and the other cheerleaders ran on. Kate signaled for the cheer called "Determination":

> "Determination, ability
> Eagles are after victory
> Hey, Warriors
> Watch out!"

On the word "out," Zoe and the other girls did their routine. The crowd went wild.

Exhausted, Zoe collapsed on the bench to watch the last play before the half. The Warriors scored another three-point basket with the stolen ball. Now the Eagles were ahead by only four points. But there was no time to worry about losing. If Zoe and Minda were to have any time at all with Ethan and Jeremy during the game, they had to move fast.

A couple minutes later, the girls had scaled

the bleachers and were standing with Jeremy and Ethan. "I know the secret," Jeremy told them smugly.

"What secret?" Minda demanded. She raised her hands menacingly. "I'm warning you, I'll tickle it out of you if I have to."

"You don't need to," said Ethan. He put his arm around Zoe and gave her a little squeeze. "I'll tell you where we're going tonight."

Zoe tipped back her head and looked up into Ethan's dark eyes. She felt sure she could go anywhere he suggested and have a wonderful time just because he was there.

"We're going to Cafe Gilbert," Ethan said. "Ever heard of it?"

"You mean that coffeehouse on the junior college campus?" Minda didn't look exactly thrilled. Zoe knew she had probably been hoping they were going to a party or at least someplace where they could dance.

"Ethan's playing there tonight," Jeremy said.

"Playing what?" Zoe said.

"The banjo!" Jeremy exclaimed. "Isn't that a hoot?" Several kids sitting around them looked their way curiously. "Ethan plays the banjo and he's playing on their open stage tonight."

Ethan's face turned red. At moments like

this, Zoe thought, he almost did seem shy. But he wasn't really shy. He was just a very private person. He told people what he wanted them to know and that was that. Zoe was certain he had other secrets besides his banjo playing, and she couldn't help wondering how many of those secrets he planned on sharing with her—and when.

"I can't wait to hear you play. Do you sing, too?" Zoe asked as the high school chorus line, the Edenettes, trotted onto the gym floor for the halftime show.

"I'll let you be the judge of that," Ethan said. He picked up one of her hands and held it between both of his. "I hope you don't mind. I thought since you'd been performing for me during the game, I'd perform for you afterward. You *have* been cheering just for me, haven't you?" he teased.

"Of course," Zoe said matter-of-factly. She placed her free hand on top of Ethan's.

"Okay, break it up, you two," Minda commanded as the last of the Edenettes filed out of the gym to the fading background music. "We've got to get back to work, Zoe. The Eagles need us tonight. We're going to make the guys win this one or go hoarse trying!"

"Knock 'em dead!" said Jeremy. He made a victory sign with his fingers.

Zoe and Minda joined the rest of the squad running back and forth in front of the bleachers, waving their gold-and-white pompons and chanting, "Go! Fight! Win!" Then the teams came onto the court and everyone on both sides of the gym went wild. It really was anyone's game, and knowing that only made it that much more exciting. Zoe cheered as loud and as hard as she could.

"I can't *believe* how great the Eagles played!" Minda said when she and Zoe went to meet the boys outside the gym after the game. The girls had changed out of their cheerleading outfits. Both were wearing jeans, and Minda had on a soft yellow sweater that complemented her blond curls. Zoe's sweater was red, her favorite color after blue.

Zoe laughed. "It really was an exciting game."

"It sure was," Minda said, stifling a yawn with the back of her hand. But Jeremy, who walked up to them just then, saw the yawn anyway.

"Don't tell me you're actually tired!" he exclaimed. Turning to Ethan, he added, "This girl has incredible stamina. She made me dance every dance at Homecoming. I thought my feet were going to fall off when the party was over, but Minda could have danced all night."

"I'm a *little* tired," Minda confessed, smiling. "But I'm ready to go!"

"Listening to Ethan perform will be restful." Jeremy gave Ethan a friendly slap on the back. "Right, buddy?"

Ethan pretended to scowl at Minda. "Just don't fall asleep. If I hear snoring in the audience, I'll probably get stage fright, and that would be worse than getting a cramp in the middle of a dive." He helped Zoe put on her tan wool coat. "Let's get going. I'm on at ten and I'd like to warm up a little before that— in more ways than one."

Jeremy and Ethan had come to the game together in Jeremy's rebuilt Chevy. Ethan and Zoe climbed in the back. Minda slid over in the front seat until she was snuggled up next to Jeremy.

"No seat belts?" Zoe asked, feeling along the backseat with her hand.

"They're there," Jeremy assured her. "But you and Ethan might want to think about sharing one. It's warmer that way."

"And friendlier, too," Minda giggled.

"I found mine," Ethan announced, pulling up the two halves.

"So did I," Zoe said, feeling a little disappointed. But a few minutes later, as Jeremy turned the car out of the parking lot, Zoe was thrilled to feel Ethan's hand on her own. Although the car was cold, Zoe felt quite warm, and she was sorry when Jeremy announced that they'd arrived.

"And here's a place to park right out front," Jeremy said.

"Isn't this a little close to the fire hydrant?" Minda asked.

"Maybe," Jeremy said cheerfully. He turned off the engine and got out.

Ethan looked at Zoe and shrugged. "If Jeremy gets towed, I'll call a cab just for us," he told her, helping Zoe out of the car. "We'll let Jeremy walk."

"Hey, what about me?" Minda pouted.

"Don't worry about it," Jeremy said. He went around to the back of the car to get Ethan's banjo out of the trunk.

The coffeehouse was run by students from the local junior college. It was very casual. Almost everyone was wearing T-shirts and worn-looking jeans. Zoe was glad she and Minda had changed. Being seen at Cafe Gilbert in a high school cheerleading outfit would have been very embarrassing.

While Ethan and Jeremy got sodas, Zoe and Minda found a table to the left of the little stage. The four of them sat and chatted for a while, then listened to several performers sing and play.

"I'm on next," Ethan whispered to Zoe as a guy with a wispy mustache and an even wispier beard got up to play three songs on a country fiddle. After introducing himself and naming the first song he was going to play, the guy began, playing at breakneck speed.

"He's good," Ethan whispered to Zoe. He sounded a little nervous, and she gave him a reassuring smile. She was sure he wouldn't be performing there if he wasn't really good on the banjo.

A few minutes later Ethan picked up his five-stringed banjo and ran onto the stage.

"Why aren't there more people here?" Zoe whispered as Ethan was tuning his instrument and adjusting the microphone.

Jeremy shrugged. "I guess only the performers' friends come to these open-stage things. And I think Ethan might be the last one scheduled tonight."

"And probably the best," Zoe stated.

Minda shook her head in wonder. "A banjo! Ethan's the only person I know who plays one of those."

"I didn't know it either," Jeremy said, "and I'm the swim-team captain. I'm supposed to know everything about all the guys on my team."

Not many people know much about Ethan Anderson, Zoe thought. *He seems to like surprises—and privacy.*

"First off," Ethan said easily, smiling at the audience, "I'm going to play 'The Arkansas Traveler.' It's a traditional banjo piece that I'm sure most of you will recognize." With that, his fingers started flying over the strings. The music was fun. Zoe realized she *did* recognize the piece, from the Saturday-morning cartoons she used to watch when she was little. It was music she associated with barnyard animals in general and chickens in particular.

"He's great!" Minda declared after the song had ended and Ethan was busy retuning his instrument. "I didn't think I'd like banjo music, but I do."

Minda sounded a little surprised that Ethan had turned out to be such a good player, but Zoe wasn't surprised at all. Ethan seemed to be the kind of boy who was good at everything he did. And he looked terrific on the stage.

Suddenly Zoe had an idea. She rummaged through her big shoulder bag and pulled out the sketch pad she always carried with her.

As soon as she found a pencil, she began doing several quick drawings of Ethan, who had begun to play again. Zoe was pleased with her efforts. So was Ethan when he saw them.

"They're great," he said as he looked at the drawings over her shoulder. He'd just returned to the table after finishing a set of three songs and an encore. "I sent the other one you did to my folks. I think I'll keep these for myself."

"You were fabulous, Ethan!" Minda exclaimed. "I actually learned something tonight. I found out that I *love* banjo music! At least, I love the way you play it."

"It's a special style," Ethan explained. Then he chuckled and said, "I won't bore you with the details. I'm glad you liked it, Minda."

Jeremy yawned. "I hate to be a party pooper," he said, yawning again, "but we have a big meet tomorrow, and I *am* the captain."

"I guess that means we should head out now," Minda said. "Since we're cheerleaders, Zoe and I can't be responsible for helping you guys break training, now can we?"

"Definitely not," Zoe agreed.

"I get the message," Ethan said. He leaned over and slipped his banjo back in its case.

He carefully rolled up Zoe's sketches and slipped them in, too.

"I'm ready," he said, giving the case an affectionate pat.

"I need to make a pit stop," Zoe said as they were on their way out. "Want to come with me, Minda?"

"Okay," Minda agreed. But when they got to the bathroom, they both started laughing. It was the size of a closet.

"I'll wait outside," Minda said, reaching for the doorknob.

Zoe caught her hand. "Wait. I don't really have to go to the bathroom. I just wanted to ask what you know about Ethan. Has Jeremy told you anything?"

Minda frowned. "I don't think I know anything you don't know. I'm not sure Jeremy does, either. Ethan seems like a pretty private guy. Why?"

"I just keep wondering why he's here in Edenvale when his family is in Arizona. From what I can tell, he doesn't even plan to go home over the holidays. But he really seems to care about his family and to hate the cold weather up here," Zoe reflected. "I can't help wondering what's going on."

"I don't know. Why don't you just ask him?"

Zoe shook her head. "If he wanted to talk about it, he would. I don't want him to think I'm snoopy. I don't want to ruin things with Ethan before they've even gotten off the ground."

"What are you so worried about?" Minda wondered. Then an idea struck her. "You mean you think Ethan's got an old girlfriend stashed away at home?" she asked, her blue eyes twinkling with amusement.

"Go ahead and laugh," Zoe said. "But something's wrong, I can tell. I just wish I could find out what. Who knows? Maybe I could even help."

Minda nodded. "Maybe you could. Well, I'll keep my eyes and ears open and if I find out anything at all, I'll let you know. Now let's get out of here. The boys are probably worrying that something's happened to us in here."

"*There* you are," Ethan said when they reached the door. He helped Zoe into her coat. "Everything okay?"

"We were getting worried," Jeremy added.

"We're fine," Minda said lightly. She looked at Zoe and winked.

A light snow was drifting down outside.

"I love these early snows," Zoe said. Ethan slipped his arm around her, and she snuggled against his side as they navigated the slippery sidewalk to Jeremy's car.

"Do you ski?" she asked Ethan as they drove home.

"I water ski," Ethan replied. "I've never tried snow skiing, but I'd like to. Do you?"

Zoe nodded. "Both downhill and cross-country."

Ethan ran a finger along Zoe's upturned nose. "Will you promise to teach me?" he asked.

Zoe shivered, and it wasn't from the cold. "I'd love to," she said. Just then Jeremy came to a stop in front of her house.

"I'll walk you to the door," Ethan said, unfastening his seat belt.

They reached the front porch of the Reilys' house in silence. Ethan put his hands on Zoe's shoulders and drew her toward him.

"I had a wonderful time," he whispered against her cheek. Her mother had forgotten to leave the front light on, so they were alone in the shadows, at least for a moment.

"I did too," Zoe said breathlessly. Then she felt his soft lips gently brushing hers and "wonderful" was no longer the right word to express what she was feeling. Ethan's arms slipped down from her shoulders. Encircling her waist, he moved even closer to her. Their kiss deepened, and Zoe knew there was only one word to describe her state. The word was love!

Chapter Six

The first thing Zoe thought when she opened her eyes Saturday morning was, *I'm in love!* She wasn't falling in it anymore—she'd arrived!

Zoe smiled, remembering how sweet Ethan's kisses had been. Her smile broadened as she remembered that she would be seeing Ethan later in the day, first at the swim meet, then again afterward. And today, they would be going out alone.

Zoe sat up in bed and stretched. *Maybe today*, she told herself, *I'll ask Ethan why he's chosen to live with his aunt and uncle instead of his parents this year.* It might turn out to be unimportant, but Zoe had the feeling that it was the key to understanding Ethan. Since she knew she loved him, that understanding seemed terribly important.

Zoe glanced over at her clock radio and gasped. She'd overslept, probably because she'd been too excited to go right to sleep after she got in the night before.

It was already ten-thirty and Minda was supposed to pick Zoe up at eleven. *How*, she asked herself, *am I going to eat, get dressed for the meet and my date with Ethan, and do all my Saturday-morning chores in half an hour?* She remembered that it was her turn this week to clean the bathrooms, a long, tedious job.

Zoe leaped out of bed and quickly slipped out of her pink cotton nightshirt. *I can skip breakfast just this once*, she told herself as she rummaged frantically through her sweater drawer for something to wear.

She selected a melon-colored turtleneck with a pattern of black circles outlined in yellow. As she slipped the sweater over her head, she decided that the bathrooms could be gone over quickly. She'd do a more thorough job when she got home later.

Zoe grabbed a pair of black jeans out of her drawer and struggled to pull them on. Obviously, Tara had put them in the dryer last week when it had been her turn to do the wash. Zoe took a deep breath and sucked in her stomach as she forced the zipper up. After several quick deep knee bends, the jeans felt a little more comfortable. Zoe smiled at her reflection in the full-length mirror on her closet door. She decided she looked pretty good in the tight jeans, and at the moment looking good was more important than feeling perfectly comfortable. Maybe she should thank Tara instead of chewing her out.

Zoe grabbed her brush and dashed down the hall to the bathroom she shared with her sister. She was washing her face when she heard Tara come in.

"Hi, Zoe," Tara said in a muffled voice.

"Hi," Zoe said, her eyes tightly closed to prevent the soap from getting into them. She rinsed the soap off, then reached for a towel and patted her face dry.

She was just turning to hang up the towel when she heard Tara sniffling. Her little sister was crying.

"Tara!" Zoe exclaimed, going over to her. "What's wrong?" She couldn't remember seeing Tara look so devastated since their father's plane had taken off for Australia.

Tara shook her head. Another tear ran

slowly down her cheek. "Dad called last night," she finally managed to choke out.

Panicked, Zoe grabbed one of her sister's arms. "Is he hurt? Where is he?"

"He's still in Australia," Tara said between sobs. "He was going to come home, but only for a couple weeks. Now he's not coming home at all."

"Not ever?" Zoe gasped.

"I don't know for sure," Tara said. "But that's the way it sounded to me."

Zoe felt as if she'd been slapped. There was a large lump caught in her throat that was making it difficult for her to breathe. "Where's Mom?" she asked her sister.

"Mom went into her room last night right after Dad called," Tara said, sniffling again. "She hasn't come out since. Zoe, I'm scared. Mom and Dad must be getting a divorce or something. I'm afraid we're never going to see Dad again!"

Zoe poked her head out of the bathroom and looked down the hall at her mother's closed bedroom door.

"What should we do?" Tara whispered.

Before Zoe could think of something comforting to say for both Tara and herself, the doorbell rang.

Tara looked even more upset. "Who's that?" she asked.

"It must be Minda," Zoe said. "We're—we *were* going to the swim meet together." Suddenly Ethan and the swim meet seemed very remote, almost unimportant. The doorbell rang again. "I've got to go down and let her in, Tara."

Tara sighed. "Okay." Zoe looked at her sister's face with concern. There were dark circles under Tara's hazel eyes, and she suddenly looked much older than twelve. "I'm going back to my room," Tara said wearily.

Zoe ran downstairs to open the door.

"Hurry up!" Minda said, smiling eagerly and shaking snow off her boots. "If we get there early, we can talk to the boys before the meet starts."

"I'm not sure I'm going," Zoe said faintly.

"What?" Minda asked, astonished. She stepped in.

Zoe slowly closed the door. She felt strangely detached, as if nothing that was happening was quite real.

Minda narrowed her blue eyes as she peered into Zoe's brown ones. "You're not sick, are you?" she asked anxiously.

Zoe shook her head. "Come into the kitchen with me." Once they were sitting at the round maple table, Zoe murmured, "It looks like my father's not coming home." She lowered her head into her hands. "He called last night after you picked me up for the basketball game."

"You mean he's not coming home in time for the holidays?" Minda asked cautiously.

Zoe shook her head again. "According to Tara, not ever. Mom hasn't come out of her room since he called, and Tara's pretty freaked out."

"Gee, that's awful," Minda said sympathetically. "I guess you should stay then, although I'm not sure why. I mean, what good can you do around here?"

"Probably none," Zoe admitted. "But I can't just leave Tara when she's so upset."

"I understand," Minda said, standing up. "Don't worry. I'll explain everything to Ethan."

"Don't tell Ethan," Zoe said quickly. "It's too embarrassing."

"It isn't your fault," Minda reasoned. "There's nothing for you to be embarrassed about."

"Still . . ." Zoe's voice trailed off. She couldn't put the way she felt into words. It might not be her fault, but her family was falling apart, and she didn't want anyone to know about it.

"I have to tell him something," Minda said. She started toward the door.

"Just tell him I'm having a family problem. Tell him it's no big deal, and I'll talk to him later," Zoe said. "Make sure he knows this has nothing to do with him or my feelings about him."

"Sure you won't change your mind?" Minda asked.

Zoe sighed. "I wish I could, but I can't."

"Okay. I'll call you." Minda hurried out the door and ran all the way to her brother's car. Zoe knew Minda was uncomfortable with depressing problems, and Zoe's problem at the moment was definitely depressing. Both her mother and her sister were behind closed doors, probably crying, and her father was half a world away with apparently no intention of coming back.

Zoe wandered around the kitchen, but after opening the cupboard and staring at its contents for several minutes, she found that eating was the last thing she wanted to do. The shock she'd felt at first was giving way to anger. She was furious at her father for abandoning the family like this.

Zoe went to the cleaning-supplies closet

and got out all the supplies she needed to clean the bathrooms. Viciously scrubbing tile and polishing mirrors seemed like a constructive way for her to vent her anger. In just a little over an hour, all two and a half bathrooms sparkled and Zoe felt a little better. But her mother and sister were still in their rooms.

Zoe put the cleaning supplies away and got out the dustcloths and furniture polish. When she had finished polishing the furniture she got out the vacuum cleaner. By one o'clock, all the Saturday-morning cleaning chores were done and Zoe decided to reward herself with a long, hot shower.

Half an hour later, feeling more relaxed and not nearly as angry, Zoe began to feel hungry. She headed down to the kitchen for something to eat, wearing her cozy terry robe with her hair wrapped in a towel, turban-style.

"Mom!" Zoe exclaimed when she discovered her mother, dressed in jeans and a sweater, sitting calmly at the kitchen table, sipping coffee.

"Hi, dear," Mrs. Reily said, glancing up and smiling as though everything were perfectly normal. "Did you do all the cleaning yourself today?"

Zoe nodded as she crossed the room and sat down across from her mother. "Yes, I did. It felt good. I was really mad when Tara told me about Dad—mad at Dad." She put her hand on her mother's. "Everything is going to be all right. I mean, it's not as if we haven't been getting along fine without him for the last three months." Zoe meant to sound encouraging, but she realized her voice sounded bitter.

If her mother noticed, though, she didn't show it. "I wish it were that simple, honey," she said. "But the truth is, it's not. These kinds of things never are. From your father's point of view, *I'm* the villain."

"*You!*" Zoe gasped. "That's really unfair!"

Mrs. Reily sighed. "Oh, Zoe, thank you for taking my side. That's really sweet of you. The trouble is, there really aren't any sides to take. In a way, your father's right. In another way, he isn't. But things will work out in the end. I really do believe that."

"Do you still love him, Mom?" Zoe asked softly.

"Of course I love him, but love can't always solve problems, Zoe. In fact, sometimes love makes things like this even harder."

Zoe wanted to ask her mother to explain, but for some reason she couldn't think of the right words to use. She felt as if her brain were tied up in knots.

Tara came downstairs and joined them.

"Come here, honey," their mother said. She held out her arms and Tara flung herself into them. The two of them were still hugging when the phone rang.

"I'll get it," Zoe said. She crossed the kitchen and picked up the wall phone. "Hello."

"Zoe? It's Ethan. Is everything all right? Is there anything I can do?" he asked. His voice was filled with concern. More than anything, Zoe wanted to see him and to be with him.

But she forced herself to sound calm as she said, "We're fine. How are you? How was the meet?"

"I missed hearing you cheer for me," he replied, "but we won anyway."

Zoe actually laughed. "You probably got all nines on your dives, too."

"No. But I did get a couple of sevens," he admitted. "That doesn't mean I didn't miss you, though. It just means I managed to carry on without you."

"That's nice to hear," she said softly. "That you missed me, I mean. I missed you, too."

"Can you come out for a while?" he asked. "We could get something to eat."

Zoe glanced at her mother and sister. They didn't seem to be paying any attention to her phone call.

"That would be nice," Zoe said. "Let me just make sure it's okay with my mom. I'll call you back. Where are you?"

"I'm still at school. I'd better call you back." Ethan sounded as eager as Zoe felt. They agreed to speak again in ten minutes.

Zoe hung up the phone. "That was Ethan Anderson," Zoe told her mother. "He wants to take me out for something to eat. The Eagles won the swim meet," she added, realizing as soon as she'd spoken how trivial the swim team's record was compared to what was happening to her family. "Do you mind if I go?"

"I think that's a fine idea," Mrs. Reily said. "We've all done entirely too much moping around today. Tara and I are going to go out, too."

"We are?" Tara looked surprised. "Why?"

Mrs. Reily shrugged. "Why not? Thanks to Zoe, the house is clean. We all deserve a little fun." She stood up. "Come on, girls. Let's get ready!"

Twenty minutes later, Ethan picked Zoe up at her house in his cousin's Toyota. He took them to the Edenvale Diner, where they sat in a booth in the back, waiting for their extra-thick banana malts and burger baskets to arrive. In spite of Zoe's intention to keep her family's problems to herself, Ethan's concern and gentle prodding had succeeded in getting her to tell him the whole story.

"He's got to come home sometime," Ethan pointed out.

"Not if he doesn't want to." Zoe sighed.

"But maybe he does want to. Want my advice?" Ethan asked.

"That depends," she said as she slowly raised her eyes to his.

"On what?" Ethan asked, smiling.

"On your credentials, of course," Zoe countered, returning his smile as best she could.

"Why do I have the feeling that you're about to ask me for another installment of my life story?" he asked.

"Because you're a very perceptive person," she told him. "But I guess you know that."

Ethan settled back into the leather bench seat and looked at Zoe. "Okay, then. Ask me anything you want."

"Why did you leave home?" she asked immediately, before her courage could fail her. The question seemed more important than ever now. Zoe had a feeling that Ethan's family had gone through similar problems when Ethan had made his decision to leave Arizona. Understanding Ethan's reasons for leaving home might help her understand her father's position.

Ethan looked down at the table. "I had lots of reasons," he said evasively.

"Such as?" Zoe asked.

Ethan raised his head. "Okay. I can see you're not going to let me off the hook. I'll give you one of my reasons, a big one. My folks were too protective. Like smothering. They were driving me nuts. Meanwhile, my little sister needed their attention, and they were both ignoring her. Now that I'm out of the picture, Sarah Jeanne is getting all the attention she can take. My aunt doesn't try to mother me." Ethan grinned. "She's too busy with Doug."

"That sounds kind of hard on your parents," Zoe said. She couldn't help thinking of her own parents. Her mother was protective, but Zoe had never felt smothered by her. Then again, Mrs. Reily was pretty wrapped up in her career at the moment. Maybe her father felt neglected. Could that be the reason he wasn't coming home?

"I guess," Ethan agreed. "But it was for the best, believe me." He reached across the table and took Zoe's hand. "There's more to it than just that, but I don't really like to talk about it too much. Talking about it somehow makes it seem simpler than it is."

Zoe smiled a little. "You sound like my mother. She told me whatever is going on with my father isn't simple. She also said that love sometimes makes things harder. I guess I don't know what she means."

Ethan started to say something, but the waitress interrupted him. She put a huge silver malt shaker in front of each of them, set malt glasses next to the shakers, and gave them long-handled spoons and straws.

"Enjoy," she said with a smile. "I'll be back in a minute with your burger baskets."

Zoe took a long drink of her malt. "Families." She sighed.

"Yeah," Ethan said. "Parents in general and mothers in particular. Why don't we change the subject?"

"Okay," Zoe agreed. She took another sip of her malt. "What should we talk about?"

"Art?" Ethan suggested. "Music?"

"Either one is fine. But first, could I ask you one more question? Why aren't you going home for the holidays? Your parents must want you to."

Ethan nodded. "They do. And I really haven't

decided one way or the other yet. To be honest, I keep changing my mind."

"You'll have to make up your mind soon," Zoe pointed out gently.

"I know," Ethan said. His eyes had a faraway look and suddenly Zoe felt lonely. Though she still hadn't found out what she wanted to know, she decided it really was time to change the subject.

Chapter Seven

"Is this project going to get us an A?" Jennifer demanded the following day. She put her hands on her hips and gazed critically at the squares of paraffin next to the wooden cigar box on the Reilys' kitchen counter.

Zoe shrugged. "I'd be happy with a B."

"Not me. Getting a B would lower my English grade," Jennifer declared.

"It was your idea to make wax tablets, remember?" Zoe snapped. She felt grumpy. This was the last way she wanted to spend a Sunday afternoon.

Jennifer smiled. "That's right. It was, wasn't it? Well, it's not such a bad idea. Our assignment was to make something connected with daily life in ancient Rome. The Romans used wax tablets in their schools." She picked up the wooden cigar box and waggled it at Zoe. "You watch. We'll get that A!"

"I don't care about the grade," Zoe said. "I just want to get it over with." She had already told Jennifer that her father wasn't coming home, and Jennifer had been sympathetic. But she'd insisted that keeping busy was the best way to handle a crisis.

"Why don't you volunteer at the hospital over winter vacation?" Jennifer had asked for the millionth time. "It will keep your mind occupied and you'll be helping people at the same time."

Zoe had accused her of being a nag, but Jennifer had just shrugged good-naturedly and let the matter drop for the moment. Then they'd gone out to the kitchen to work on the English project that had been assigned for the play *Julius Caesar*.

"Get out a saucepan," Jennifer ordered. As usual, she was taking charge, but Zoe didn't mind. She took a medium-sized aluminum saucepan out of the cupboard and set it on the front burner of the stove.

"Better set the burner on low. We don't want this stuff to melt too fast," Jennifer said. While Zoe turned on the burner, Jennifer started unwrapping the blocks of paraffin and dropping them into the pan.

"I'll get a spoon," Zoe said.

When she returned with the spoon, Jennifer took it and said, "So how's Ethan?"

At the mention of Ethan's name, Zoe smiled. She remembered how sweet he'd been yesterday. "Great," she said softly.

"Where did you go Friday night?" Jennifer asked. "The last time I talked to you, it was a big mystery."

"It's funny. Friday night seems like years ago," Zoe said ruefully. "We went to the Cafe Gilbert. You know, that coffeehouse at the junior college. Ethan played the banjo on their stage."

Jennifer stared at her. "Ethan plays the *banjo*?"

Zoe nodded. "He's really good, too. He's actually kind of a ham."

"Oh, Zoe! You've got to talk him into playing at the holiday party at the hospital! The kids would adore it. It would be wonderful!"

"He may be going to Arizona over vacation," Zoe said. "Anyway, he's thinking about going, and I think he should. Families ought to be together for the holidays."

"At least ask him," Jennifer said. She looked at Zoe for a minute, then shook her head. "Forget it. I'll ask him myself." Jennifer handed Zoe the spoon. "Stir that stuff. If you don't, it might catch fire. I've got a phone call to make."

As Zoe stared at her, open-mouthed, Jennifer hurried to the wall phone and punched the numbers for directory assistance.

"Information?" Jennifer said. "I'd like the number of the Andersons on Lake Terrace."

"How do you know what street Doug Anderson lives on?" Zoe demanded, crossing the kitchen to stand next to Jennifer as she scribbled down the phone number the operator was giving her. But Jennifer didn't answer.

After Jennifer had dialed the number, Zoe heard her say, "Hello? Is this Doug? . . . Hi, Doug. This is Jennifer Lund. I met you at the mall last week, remember?"

Zoe leaned back against the wall next to the phone and groaned faintly. She couldn't believe her friend was doing this!

Jennifer continued to make small talk with Ethan's cousin. She finally got around to asking, "Is Ethan there? . . . Well, can I talk to him?" Jennifer looked at Zoe and rolled her eyes toward the ceiling as if to say, "How dense can you be?"

A moment later, she said, "Hi, Ethan. This

is Jennifer Lund. I was wondering—" But before she could finish, Zoe grabbed the phone away from her. "Hi. It's Zoe, too," she said.

"What's going on?" Ethan asked, sounding puzzled.

Zoe sighed. "Jennifer just found out that you play the banjo. She's determined to have you play for her holiday party at the Children's Hospital. If you're going to be around for the holidays, that is."

"A little winter solstice music?" Ethan said. Zoe was glad that he sounded amused.

"Right," she said, leaning back against the wall. Her glance fell to the pan of paraffin on the stove. "Oh, my gosh!" she cried. "It's on fire!" Without thinking, she hung up the phone and ran to the stove.

"A wet towel!" Jennifer said as she turned off the burner. "Get a wet towel, quick!"

Frantically, Zoe pulled a dish towel from the rack beneath the sink and soaked it. Jennifer snatched it from her and draped it over the pan.

The towel did the trick. The fire was out. Zoe was grateful that Jennifer had thought of it. But then she realized that the paraffin probably would never have burned if Jennifer hadn't impulsively decided to call Ethan.

"Oh, my gosh!" Zoe cried, her hand flying up to cover her mouth. "I hung up on him!"

"Not too much damage," Jennifer said cheerfully. "The pan is ruined, of course, and there's a little black mark on the cupboard over the stove. . . ."

Zoe examined the cupboard. "Oh, great," she said despondently. "Mom's going to love this." She sank into the nearest chair. The last thing her poor mother needed right now, in addition to everything else, was a burned cupboard!

The doorbell rang. The girls exchanged panicked looks.

"Your mother?" Jennifer's eyes were as big as saucers.

"Of course not," Zoe said. "She'd just use her key and come in. I'll go see who it is." She started toward the front of the house.

"Ethan!" she cried as she opened the front door. His hair was dusted with snow and his dark eyes looked frantic with worry.

"Are you all right?" he asked. "I heard you say something about fire, and then you hung up. I didn't know what to think, so I decided to come right over."

"I'm sorry. Everything's okay," Zoe said, feeling a little foolish. "Come on in—maybe you can help Jennifer and me figure out how to deal with the damage."

"No big deal," Ethan declared after examining the singed cupboard. "It's just soot. There's no real damage to the wood. Got some kitchen cleaner? You know, the spray-on stuff?"

Zoe found a can of spray cleaner under the sink and brought it to him along with a scouring pad.

"We can't use that pad," Ethan declared. "It'll scratch the paint."

Jennifer patted Ethan on the shoulder. "I like this guy," she told Zoe. "He's obviously got a practical head on his shoulders."

"Let's just say my knowledge is the kind that comes from experience. I set a pan of grease on fire once when I was trying to make pancakes to surprise my mother on Mother's Day. I surprised her, all right!" He laughed. "It's a family joke now."

Jennifer got some paper towels and brought them to Ethan. Using the spray cleaner, he was able to reduce the black to a faint brown stain.

"Not perfect," Jennifer decided. "But an awful lot easier to explain, don't you think?"

"What about our English project?" Zoe asked.

Jennifer shrugged. "We need more paraffin."

"I'm not melting any more paraffin," Zoe said firmly. "At least, not here."

"Let's take a doughnut break and think about it," Jennifer suggested. "I brought a dozen chocolate-covered doughnuts with me," she told Ethan. "Want some?"

Ethan said, "My favorite. Got any milk?" he asked Zoe.

Zoe opened the refrigerator. "It looks like there's two cartons in here."

"That'll do," Jennifer said. She opened a cupboard and got out three glasses.

Once they were sitting around the Reilys' kitchen table with their milk and doughnuts, Jennifer turned to Ethan. "So what have you decided? Are you going to entertain my kids or not?"

"Despite appearances, Jennifer's going to be a pediatrician, not a trial lawyer," Zoe explained dryly. "She takes volunteering at Children's very seriously."

"I admire that," Ethan said. "And I've decided I'll definitely help out at the party."

"Will you play the banjo, too?" Jennifer asked. "The kids would really love that."

Ethan nodded. "Until somebody asks me to stop."

"That's wonderful!" Jennifer cried.

"Aren't you going to Arizona during vacation?" Zoe asked. She couldn't help feeling concerned for Ethan's family, especially now that her own family was divided.

"I'm doing that, too." Ethan reached across the table and covered Zoe's hand with his own. "You helped me decide that it was the right thing to do. But I'm not going until the twenty-third, and I'll be back on the thirtieth. I don't want to miss too many swimming practices, and I want to see you as much as possible. Will you spend New Year's Eve with me, Zoe?"

Jennifer shifted uncomfortably in her chair. "Maybe I should leave you two alone," she mumbled.

"You're invited to spend New Year's Eve with us, too, Jennifer," Ethan said, giving her one of his heart-melting smiles. "Doug's having a huge party and I'm sure he's going to ask you to come."

"I don't know," Jennifer said hesitantly. Despite all her bravado on behalf of the hospital, Jennifer was actually rather shy.

"Okay, Jennifer Lund," Zoe said. "Let's make a deal."

"Shoot," Jennifer said.

"I'll help out at the party at the hospital if you'll go to Doug's party. What do you say?"

"What can I say but yes? On one condition, that is," Jennifer countered.

Zoe looked at Ethan and shook her head. "See what I've had to put up with for the last eight years? A demanding best friend!" Turning back to Jennifer, Zoe asked, "What's the condition?"

"You have to do cartoons of the kids. They'll love it!" Jennifer said eagerly. "You could also lead them in a few get-well cheers."

"But don't upstage my banjo playing," Ethan warned her with a grin.

"Okay, it's a deal," Zoe said.

Jennifer reached for the doughnut bag. "How about one more doughnut to cement this deal?"

"I could go for that," Ethan agreed.

"I'll get some more milk," Zoe said.

While she took the carton from the refrigerator, she reflected that this part of her life was perfect. Her father might have let the family down, but she had terrific friends and a fabulous boyfriend. In spite of everything else that was wrong, Zoe couldn't help feeling happy.

Chapter Eight

"I should never have said I'd do it, Minda," Zoe said. She rolled onto her back and transferred the phone from one ear to the other as she glanced out her bedroom window. The gray December sky fit her mood.

It was Sunday, the second day of winter vacation, and it was snowing again. But Zoe wasn't happy about either, at least not as happy as she might have been. Tomorrow was the party at Children's Hospital, and Zoe was dreading it. Even the promise of enough snow for skiing and enough vacation time to do it in didn't cheer her up.

"Tell Jennifer something's come up," suggested Minda. "Tell her you have to go somewhere with your mom."

"I couldn't." Zoe sighed. "Jennifer would be really mad. Of course, she's been mad at me before." She sat up and began coiling the phone cord around her index finger. Minda's idea was tempting, but impossible. "No," she said with another sigh. "I can't back out now. You heard what Ethan said on the way home from our double date last night. He said he couldn't wait for me to hear the banjo music he's put together for the party. He's really taking it seriously, like it's very important to him. He's almost as bad as Jennifer about it."

"So tell him about your aunt. Ethan seems like a really understanding guy," Minda pointed out. "I'm sure he'd see how an experience like that could upset you so much that you'd never want to walk into a hospital again."

"That's the problem," Zoe replied. "Ethan's such a wonderful person that if something like that happened to someone in his family, I'm sure he'd have exactly the opposite reaction. He'd probably spend every spare minute at some hospital helping to cheer up the patients instead of avoiding them. But I'm the kind of person sick people complain about, the kind who makes them feel worse instead of better. If I go, Ethan is bound to see that. Either way, he's going to think less of me after this. I'm doomed!"

"Want me to ask Jeremy to tell Ethan you can't make it to the party?" Minda offered. "I'm sure Jeremy would do it."

"Oh, no. That would be worse than telling Ethan myself. I guess I'll just have to go and try not to freak out. I'll tell you one thing, though. I'll be glad when the party is finally over," Zoe said.

"Now that you're going for sure, what are you going to wear?" Minda asked. She was always eager to discuss clothes.

"I haven't gotten that far." Zoe fell back against the pile of pillows at the head of her bed. "Maybe I better call Jennifer for some ideas."

"Okay. I can take a hint," Minda said with a chuckle. "You want me to hang up."

"For now. But don't go too far from the phone," Zoe pleaded. "You're the only person I can really talk to about this. Jennifer knows, but she just doesn't understand. I may need to keep calling for moral support."

Minda said, "I feel the same way about hospitals and I never even knew somebody who died in one. I think you're pretty brave for sticking with this thing. I'd have bailed out long ago, I'm sure of it."

"Thanks, Minda," Zoe told her. "You've made me feel a lot better."

"That's what friends are for, right?"

The girls exchanged good-byes. Then Zoe dialed Jennifer's number.

"I'll be wearing my volunteer outfit," Jennifer said in answer to the clothes question. "But you can wear whatever you want. I'd suggest pants, though. Kids are messy, and you might end up on the floor with a few of them in your lap."

"Uh, all right," Zoe said uneasily. While she'd been talking to Minda, she'd almost convinced herself that she could handle going to the party. But now that she was talking to Jennifer, she was starting to think that maybe she couldn't handle it after all. The thought of having sick little kids crawling all over her made her cringe.

"Having second thoughts?" Jennifer asked. She and Zoe had been friends for so long that Jennifer could often tell what Zoe was thinking.

"Yes, I am," Zoe admitted. "But I'm not going to back out," she added hastily.

Jennifer paused. "Maybe you should," she said at last.

"Are you serious? I thought you'd kill me if I did that!" Zoe exclaimed.

"Actually, I was sort of hoping you'd get over this phobia of yours. But if you're not going to . . . I guess I should just come right out and say what's on my mind, right?"

"Okay," Zoe said.

"The truth is, I don't want to ruin this party for the kids," Jennifer said. "I mean, I love you like a sister, Zoe, but if you're nervous and they get uncomfortable, then maybe it's not such a good idea. So maybe you'd better just stay home."

Zoe swallowed hard. "I won't make them uncomfortable, I promise." Zoe couldn't believe she was actually pleading with Jennifer to let her go to the party—the very same party she had just been telling Minda she wanted to get out of!

"Some of these kids have lost their hair because of cancer treatment," Jennifer went on. "Some of them are awfully pale and thin. And some of them have tubes running in and out of their noses and stuff. I mean, you're going to have to see beyond all that."

"I can do that," Zoe murmured, feeling terribly afraid even as she said it. But she couldn't stand the idea that Ethan would think she was a wimp, or worse yet, that she didn't care about the sick children.

"Okay," Jennifer finally said. "You can come then. Wear something bright. The kids like bright colors. You might even wear your cheerleading outfit. They'd all love that."

After Zoe hung up the phone, she sat in stunned silence. What had she done? Jennifer had bent over backwards to give her an out, and she had refused to take it.

Zoe stood up and crossed her bedroom to her dresser. She picked up her father's picture. "*I'm* not a quitter," she told the handsome face with gentle brown eyes—eyes so like her own—that looked out of the silver frame. "*I* don't run away from my commitments. I'm no coward!"

When Zoe set her father's picture back down, she was suddenly overwhelmed by anger. If it weren't for her father, she wouldn't have to prove herself like this. She could have been honest with Jennifer. She probably could have been honest with Ethan, too.

But then, Zoe thought, *I might have ended up like my father, running away as soon as things get tough, hiding out on the other side of the world.* He had called early that morning. Zoe's mother had said he wanted to talk to her, but Zoe had really had nothing to say to him—at least, nothing nice. Her thoughts were interrupted by a knock on the door.

"Who is it?" Zoe called.

"It's Mom. Can I come in?"

"Sure."

Mrs. Reily opened the door and came into the room. "Hi. I think we need to talk, honey."

"If it's about Dad, Mom, forget it," Zoe said quickly. "As far as I'm concerned, he deserted us and that's all there is to it."

Mrs. Reily looked upset. "But that's just it, Zoe. You've made a mistake somehow. You don't have the whole picture. Dad hasn't deserted us," her mother insisted.

"Where is he, then?" Zoe looked around the room. "I don't see him." She knew she was being hard on her mother, but there was no one else to vent her anger on. Tara had been acting so sad for the past week that Zoe had gone out of her way to be nicer to her than usual. In a strange way, Zoe felt closer to her sister than she'd ever felt before. It was as if they were on the same team for a change instead of being competitors.

Her mother sat down on the bed. "I guess you've forgotten that Dad wanted us all to go to Australia with him when this business trip first came up. But I had my work. You see, I put my career goals on hold while you and Tara were little, Zoe. I did it because I wanted to, and I don't regret it. But if I dropped everything again for a few months in Australia, I knew I'd never go back to it. I didn't want that to happen. I had to stick to my dream despite Dad's plans."

"What are you saying, Mom? Are you telling me that you're responsible for splitting up with Dad?" Zoe asked, confused.

Her mother shook her head. "No. Because there hasn't really been any split-up, honey. Dad will be coming home again, I'm sure of it."

"When?" Zoe demanded, planting her hands on her hips. "In the spring? In the summer? Next year?"

"When his work is done," Mrs. Reily said evenly. "I wish you'd talked to him, honey. He feels terrible about all this. He's especially upset about the way you're taking it. But he can't give up his work any more than I can give up mine. We really do love each other and you and Tara. But neither of us could make a sacrifice right now and neither of us could give up our dreams. I really wouldn't want your father to do that for me and he wouldn't want me to do that for him. Feeling that way is part of love, too."

"But what about *us*?" Zoe was still angry. "What about Tara and me? Don't we count for anything?"

"That's why Dad called. He wanted to ask you and Tara to go there. He did ask Tara, and Tara's decided to go. Dad has a good-sized apartment in Sydney. If you decide to go, too, you'll both be able to have your own rooms."

"But what about you?" Zoe asked.

Mrs. Reily smiled. "I'll miss you, but I'll be fine. I'll be too busy to mope around feeling lonely."

Just then, Tara ran into Zoe's room.

"Isn't it great?" she cried, smiling as if the awful events of the past week had never happened. "I'm going to leave for Australia the day after New Year's!"

"You're both nuts!" Zoe said, scowling at her mother and sister.

Mrs. Reily stood up. Putting her arm around Tara, she walked with her younger daughter toward the bedroom door. "Think about it, honey, okay? Whatever you decide is fine with me. I just want you to know that both your father and I love you very much. Both of us want you with us. We realize that you have special things here you might not want to give up just now. On the other hand, finishing out the school year in Australia with Dad would be a very exciting adventure and one that might not come around again. Before you know it, we'll all be together again."

Zoe's mother and Tara left the room, shutting Zoe's door behind them. Zoe stared at the closed door for a minute. Then she threw a pillow at it. Go to Australia? Just like that? Her whole family had gone crazy!

"Zoe," Mrs. Reily called up the stairs Monday afternoon. "Ethan's here."

Zoe stuck her head into the upstairs hall. "I'll be right down," she called. *There's absolutely no backing out now,* Zoe told herself as she struggled with the breathless, nervous feeling that had been gripping her all morning. As soon as she went downstairs, Ethan would whisk her out to the car. They'd go over to the Lunds' to pick up Jennifer, and in almost no time at all, they would be entering Children's Hospital.

Zoe took one last look at herself in the mirror above her dresser. Her hair was freshly washed and shiny, and the bright red pull-over she was wearing over her jeans cast a rosy glow onto her pale cheeks.

"I look great," Zoe told her reflection mournfully. "But I feel awful." Taking one last deep breath, she started down the hall.

"I've been reading up on it," Zoe heard Tara tell Ethan excitedly. "There are all sorts of animals in Australia that aren't found anywhere else in the world, except in zoos."

Zoe sighed. Tara had really gone overboard with enthusiasm for Australia and everything Australian, and Zoe wanted to strangle her.

"I'm here," Zoe said, bounding down the stairs, interrupting Tara's lengthy list of Australia's lesser-known marsupials.

"You look great," Ethan said with a grin. "Red is definitely your color, Zoe. And it just happens to be my favorite color, too."

Zoe hurried to the closet and grabbed her ski jacket. "I'm ready," she said as she slipped it on.

"Guess I'll have to hear more about Australia another time," Ethan told Tara.

"Well," Tara said, "it better be sometime soon, because I'm leaving right after New Year's, and I don't know when I'll be back."

Ethan's dark eyebrows shot up. "You're kidding! You're actually going to Australia?"

"I really am. Isn't it great?" said Tara, grinning.

Ethan nodded. "It sure is. I'm jealous."

Zoe grabbed Ethan's hand. "Come on," she said impatiently. If she heard one more word about Australia, she was going to scream. "Jennifer will think we're not coming."

"Have fun," Mrs. Reily said as they started out the door.

"Where's your drawing paper?" Ethan asked Zoe suddenly.

"Upstairs," Zoe said with a groan. "Don't move," she told him. "I'll be right back!"

". . . and there are kangaroos all over the place," Tara was saying when Zoe came back down again.

"Bye," Zoe said, pulling Ethan outside.

"Bye, kids," Mrs. Reily called after them. Tara waved enthusiastically. *Tara's really like a completely different person*, Zoe thought. She hardly recognized her little sister.

"You're really in a hurry, aren't you?" Ethan commented as they fastened their seat belts.

"Mostly to get out of there," Zoe admitted. "My whole family has gone crazy!"

"I like your mother and sister, at least what I've seen of them so far." Ethan looked over at Zoe and smiled. "If they're crazy, that's okay with me."

114

Zoe shook her head. "I used to think I had the perfect family. But lately it's like a bomb went off in the middle of our house. Ever since Dad's company sent him to Australia, it's like we aren't even a family anymore. And the strangest thing of all is that no one else seems to think it's weird for Dad to be living thousands of miles away and for Tara to be joining him. Everyone's happy about the whole thing. Everyone except me."

Ethan backed the car out onto the street and began to drive to Jennifer's house. "Maybe that's because there isn't anything wrong with what's happening," he said. The car picked up speed. "There are two kinds of perfect, you know," Ethan went on. "There's the kind where everything happens just the way you think it should, like in a fairy tale or something."

Zoe nodded. She knew about that kind. "So what's the other kind?"

"The other kind is harder to take, and harder to like," Ethan said.

"What do you mean?"

"The other kind of perfect is when things happen the way they were meant to," Ethan replied.

Zoe frowned. "You mean like fate or something?"

"Something like that."

"Then, according to that theory, having my father not come home the way he was supposed to was the second kind of perfect," Zoe said. Her voice sounded almost accusing.

"That's right." If Ethan heard the challenge in her tone, he ignored it. "Because now all sorts of interesting things are going to happen that would never have happened if your father had come home on schedule. And a lot of those things will be good."

"But they won't all be good," Zoe pointed out.

"True." Ethan patted Zoe's mittened hand. "Life doesn't come with any guarantees."

"I know that," Zoe huffed, feeling that he was patronizing her.

Ethan smiled. "Don't be mad at me, Zoe. I didn't make the rules. I just try to make sense of them."

Zoe's expression softened. "I didn't mean to snap at you, Ethan. The last thing I want to do is argue with you." Zoe glanced out the window and added, "You'd better slow down. Jennifer's street is next. Turn right at the corner."

As soon as Ethan pulled the Toyota into the Lunds' driveway, Jennifer came running out. Zoe could see the red-and-white-striped

116

apron of her volunteer uniform beneath her navy blue coat.

"Hi," Jennifer said, leaping into the backseat and slamming the door. "You're late. You'd better get going. I don't want everything to fall apart because I'm not there."

Zoe raised her eyebrows. "Modest, isn't she?" she joked.

"I may not be modest, but I'm honest. This party is my responsibility and I want it to be really special," Jennifer said. Then, leaning forward so that her chin was resting on the back of Zoe's seat, she asked, "Did you guys bring your things?"

"Things?" Zoe asked.

Ethan smiled. "I think she means your drawing stuff and my banjo."

"Well? Did you?" Jennifer prodded.

Zoe waved her sketch pad. "A hundred sheets," she said. "Brand new."

"And my banjo is in the trunk," Ethan added. "I even put new strings on it this morning."

Jennifer leaned back and sighed with relief. "Terrific!"

Zoe had never seen her friend look so frazzled. The funny thing was that Jennifer's nervousness was actually helping Zoe to relax. *Maybe*, Zoe thought, *just maybe this party isn't going to be a disaster*. After all, how could anything be bad when she was with Ethan? If there really were two kinds of perfect, as he had said, then Ethan was definitely the first kind!

Chapter Nine

"You can park in this lot, Ethan," Jennifer said when they reached the hospital. "We'll go in that door over there."

Ethan pulled into the lot and parked the car. The girls got out and waited while he took his banjo case out of the trunk. Then the three of them scaled a snowbank and hurried across the street.

"This doesn't look like a hospital," Zoe said as the electronically controlled glass door to the lobby slid open.

Jennifer laughed. "You mean because it isn't all one boring color?"

Zoe nodded. The lobby walls were bright orange and yellow. In one corner a couple of small children were climbing on a giant stuffed panda. In another part of the lobby, there were several low tables surrounded by little chairs. Elsewhere there were shelves filled with children's books and magazines, and piles of toys.

"This place actually looks like fun," Zoe commented.

"Sometimes it is," Jennifer said. "It will be today, anyway." She waved at a teenage boy on the other side of the lobby who was pulling a large gray cylinder on wheels.

"Is he a patient?" Zoe whispered as the boy returned Jennifer's wave and started walking in their direction. She wondered if the cylinder was some kind of life-support system.

Jennifer laughed. "Oh, no. That's Rick. He's another volunteer. And that's a tank of helium he's pulling for the balloons."

When the boy came up to them, Jennifer said, "Rick, these are a couple of friends of mine, Zoe and Ethan. Zoe's going to sketch the kids, and Ethan's going to play the banjo."

"I'm glad you're here," Rick said. "The kids have already started coming into the recreation room on the fourth floor, and they're really excited."

"We'd better get up there, then," Jennifer

said. She led the way to the elevators. "Is the food here yet, Rick?"

He nodded. "The giant sun cookies came out great, too. Everyone wants one." He smiled at Ethan and Zoe. "The kids decided we'd celebrate the winter solstice this year. It's so bright in the party room, it looks like June instead of December."

"It'll be perfect, really perfect," Jennifer promised Ethan and Zoe. She sounded very proud.

Ethan took Zoe's hand as the elevator doors closed. Zoe gave his hand a squeeze and smiled at him. He smiled back. Zoe decided that the party was going to be all right after all. The elevator stopped and the doors rolled open.

"Jennifer!" A little boy wearing pajamas and a Minnesota Twins baseball cap approached them in a motorized wheelchair. His thin face made his brown eyes look huge.

"Hi, Matthew," Jennifer said, bending over to give him a gentle hug. "All set for the party?"

"You bet!" he said. As he spun his chair around, Zoe noticed that he didn't have any hair under his cap. The child didn't look a bit sad, but a wave of pity washed over her all the same.

As they walked along next to Matthew's chair, he looked up at Zoe and grinned. Though Zoe felt uncomfortable, she forced herself to return his smile. She knew she shouldn't show how sorry she felt for Matthew. That would only make him feel self-conscious.

"Hi," he said. "Are you Jennifer's friend?" He reached for Zoe's hand.

"Yes," she said. "My name's Zoe."

"That's a funny name. I'm Matthew," he told her.

"Nice to meet you, Matthew," Zoe said. She glanced at Ethan, and he smiled at her reassuringly. *I can do this*, Zoe told herself as she looked back down into Matthew's trusting eyes. "Would you like me to draw your picture?" She held up her sketch pad. "I brought lots of paper with me and I'll let you keep the picture if you like it."

"Will you draw me in my hat?" he asked eagerly.

"Why not? I can put anything you want in the picture," Zoe told him. "Anything I'm able to draw, that is."

"Can you make me a baseball player, you know, a major-league player?" Matthew demanded, sounding more and more excited.

"When I grow up, I want to be a pitcher for the Twins!"

"That's a great idea, Matthew," Zoe said. They'd reached the recreation room and Rick opened the big double doors. The cheerful, sunlit room was filled with boys and girls. Some, like Matthew, were in wheelchairs, and some were on crutches, but the rest of them were running around excitedly.

Zoe turned to Jennifer and asked, "Where should Matthew and I go to do our picture?"

"I've got a table all set up for you over there," Jennifer said, gesturing across the room.

"What about me?" Ethan asked.

"How about over there?" Jennifer pointed to the far corner. "The kids will probably drift away and come back. I thought we'd just do a lot of things all at once, sort of like a carnival."

"Sounds good to me," Ethan said agreeably. He smiled at Zoe. "Catch you later."

Zoe went over to the table with Matthew. A small crowd gathered as she worked on his drawing. All the kids were eager for Zoe to sketch them. One child wanted to be a dancer, another wanted to be a fireman, and several wanted to be drawn as doctors or nurses.

"I'm going to give this to my mom," Matthew said happily as he looked at the picture Zoe had done for him. "She'll love it." Matthew looked up at Zoe, his big eyes filled with admiration. "You're really good."

"Thanks." Zoe felt that his compliment was one of the nicest she'd ever received.

"Hey, Rick!" Matthew yelled, waving the sketch over his head as he rolled across the room. "Look at this! Isn't it cool?"

Zoe turned to the cluster of spectators. "Who's next?"

A girl who looked just a little older than Matthew said, "Me! I want to be a dancer, a ballet dancer." She too was sitting in a wheelchair, and the sight wrenched Zoe's heart.

"Okay." Zoe nodded. "Shall I draw you in toe shoes?"

The little girl beamed. "That would be perfect!"

As Zoe began to draw, she could hear Ethan's banjo music in the background over the children's happy voices. Jennifer had been right. These kids were special. Somehow their dreams seemed all the more intense because of their disabilities. And that intensity, Zoe realized, was contagious.

"Thank you," the girl said when Zoe had

finished. "It's beautiful! I'm going to hang it up right next to my bed."

"Come on, Beth," a nurse said. She smiled at Zoe as she began wheeling the child away. "Time for your medication."

"Can I come back afterward?" Beth asked.

"We'll have to see how you feel after your medication," the nurse said gently.

"Bye," Beth called over her shoulder to Zoe.

"I'm next!" a little boy shouted.

"No, I am," another boy about the same age argued.

"I won't leave until everyone has the picture he or she wants," Zoe promised. "Everyone will get a turn. Okay?"

"Darryl can go next, then," the first little boy said. "I'll go over and sing with that guy." He pointed at Ethan. When Ethan saw Zoe looking his way, he grinned at her.

"Is he your boyfriend?" An older girl named Cindy asked Zoe. Cindy was wearing a pretty flowered bathrobe with a matching scarf tied around her head. She had been watching Zoe draw ever since she started in on Matthew's baseball picture.

Zoe smiled and nodded. "Yes," she said.

"He's really cute," Cindy said. "You're so lucky!"

Zoe laughed. "I think I am too."

"I'll be back," Cindy said. "And then I want you to draw me with hair just like yours, long and reddish-brown. Make me look like a fashion model on the cover of *Teen Today*."

She went across the room and sat down with a group of kids who were singing along with Ethan's own special version of "Old MacDonald Had a Farm," which consisted of making farm-machinery noises instead of animal noises. Zoe could tell that the younger boys were especially enjoying the whirs and clicks and chugs.

"It's time for a break," Jennifer told Zoe a while later. "Come over to the refreshment table for a sun cookie before they're all gone."

"But I wanted you to do my picture!" protested a little girl named Nina.

"We'll each get a cookie," Zoe said. "Then I'll do your picture." Zoe held out her hand to Nina, who took it.

"You've been doing great," Jennifer said as the three of them crossed the room. "I'm sorry I doubted you yesterday. Having the kids tell you what they want to be when they grow up was a stroke of genius."

"It was," agreed Zoe. "But it wasn't my idea, it was Matthew's. He's really something."

"Well, whatever. I just wanted to thank you before I forgot," Jennifer said.

Zoe shook her head. "Don't thank me. I'm having as much fun as they are." She looked down at Nina and smiled. "You were right about the kids, Jen. They're really special."

"They're just kids," said Jennifer. "All kids are special." She picked up paper napkins and plates and handed them to Nina and Zoe.

"I've had a cookie already," Nina admitted. She looked hopefully at Jennifer.

"You're waiting for me to say, 'Have another one,' aren't you?" Jennifer teased, and Nina nodded solemnly.

"Nina, *dear*," Jennifer said, giving the child's nose a playful tweak, "have another one, *please!*" Nina giggled and took a cookie, then trotted off to join some other girls her age.

Remembering her promise to draw Cindy as a fashion model, Zoe began to do a quick sketch of the girl with lots of long, wavy hair.

"She'll love that," Jennifer said as she watched Zoe draw. "Cindy's thirteen and she's been really upset about losing her hair because of chemotherapy."

Zoe smiled. "Maybe flirting with Ethan will make her feel better."

"It doesn't look as if she's flirting with him," Jennifer said. "It looks like they're having some kind of serious talk, and they're gathering an audience, too." As Zoe and Jennifer watched, several other kids came over and sat down near Ethan and Cindy.

"Let's go over and find out what they're talking about," Zoe suggested. Ethan was paying serious attention to whatever Cindy was saying.

"Good idea," Jennifer agreed.

As Jennifer and Zoe started across the room, more and more kids drifted in the same direction. They all gathered around Ethan and Cindy, listening intently.

"I wonder what they're talking about," Jennifer said as they came nearer. "It must be fascinating. The kids seem to like it even more than they liked Ethan's banjo playing."

"Maybe he's telling them a story," Zoe suggested.

"*All* your hair?" Matthew was asking as the girls finally got close enough to hear.

Ethan nodded. "Every single strand. I looked like a bowling ball!"

All the kids laughed except Cindy. She reached out unselfconsciously and touched Ethan's springy dark hair. "It's so thick and curly."

Ethan smiled. "It grew back. Everyone kept saying it would but I didn't believe them. Anyway, that was almost six years ago. After five years a person's considered cured." He spread out his arms and grinned. "I'm cured."

"What on earth is he talking about?" Zoe whispered to Jennifer.

"I think Ethan's been telling them that he had cancer, too," Jennifer whispered back.

Zoe felt as if the floor had dropped out from under her. Cancer? *Ethan*? It wasn't possible! But why would he make something like that up if it weren't true? It *had* to be true! Ethan Anderson had had cancer!

"I didn't know," Zoe murmured, dazed. "He didn't tell me." Suddenly all Ethan's mysteriousness made sense. He didn't want Zoe to know he'd had cancer. He didn't want anyone to know. He'd said he'd left Arizona because his parents were too protective of him. Ethan had made it sound as if they were being unreasonable, but of course they were overprotective, Zoe realized. *Ethan could have died!* she thought. The idea made her shudder.

Zoe thought of her aunt Karen. Aunt Karen had had cancer, too. Everyone, including the doctor and Aunt Karen herself, had thought she was cured. But the cancer had come back, and the second time the doctors hadn't been able to halt its progress. What if the same thing happened to Ethan? Zoe was sure it could. She also knew she couldn't bear going through with Ethan what she'd experienced with her lovely young aunt—the fear, the loss, the grief.

"Why should he tell you?" Jennifer was saying. "If he was sick that long ago, it's over. He's cured, just like he said."

Zoe turned and headed for the door. She had to get out of the room, away from all these sick people. She needed to get some fresh air.

"Where are you going, Zoe?" Jennifer asked, following her.

"I'm going out for a minute," Zoe said. She found it hard to breathe; she felt as if all the air had suddenly been sucked out of the room. "I'll be back," she added as she stepped into the hall.

"Are you okay?" Jennifer asked worriedly, stopping in the doorway. "Should I go with you?"

Zoe shook her head and kept walking rapidly toward the elevator. When it arrived, she got on it and rode down to the first floor.

Spotting a pay phone, she hurried across the lobby and dropped in a quarter.

A moment later her mother answered. "Hello?"

"Mom? It's me. Could you pick me up at the hospital? Right away? I'm not feeling very good."

"Sure, honey, I'll be right there. Will you be in front?" her mother asked, concern in her voice.

"Yes. And please hurry!" After Zoe hung up, she realized she didn't have her coat or her sketch pad. But she wasn't going back up to get them. She couldn't. Jennifer would just have to bring her things to her later.

Zoe walked to the front of the main entrance of the hospital and waited for her mother. A few minutes later, Jennifer found her. "There you are," Jennifer said, relief in her voice. "I've been worried about—" She broke off as she saw Mrs. Reily's car pull up.

"I'm sorry, but I'm leaving, Jen." Zoe waved to her mother to let her know she'd seen her. "I have to. Bring my coat and stuff, okay?" Before Jennifer could say another word, Zoe ran to her mother's car, got in, and slammed the door. She didn't look back as the car drove away.

*   *   *

"I don't know, Zoe. I'm trying to under-stand, but I just don't get it. I was really furi-ous with you yesterday, and I'm not feeling much better today." Jennifer was standing outside the Reilys' front door, Zoe's jacket and sketch pad held tightly against her chest. The expression on her face was somewhere between anger and disgust. It was Tuesday, nearly twenty-four hours after the party at the hospital. Zoe had done a lot of thinking in that time, but she hadn't come to any con-clusions. She was too confused by her own emotions to know what to do.

"Here are your things," Jennifer said after the girls had stood staring at each other for a few seconds. With a sigh, she thrust the jacket and sketch pad at Zoe.

"Thanks," Zoe said quietly. She took them and started to close the door.

"Aren't you even going to ask me in?" Jen-nifer demanded, planting her hands on her hips. "My mom dropped me off, you know. When you opened the door she drove away. It's about fifteen degrees out here, and I'm freezing my tail off."

"I didn't think you wanted to come in," Zoe said. "I mean, I thought you were too mad at me." She opened the door wider. "Come on in."

Jennifer stepped into the front hall. "Honestly, Zoe! What got into you, anyway?" She glared at Zoe. "You were doing such a great job, then all of a sudden you ran away."

"Please don't yell at me," Zoe said. "I don't need it."

"Well, I think you need *something*," Jennifer snapped. She slipped out of her turquoise-and-white ski jacket and handed it to Zoe, who put it on the coatrack along with her own jacket.

"Want a soda or something?" Zoe asked wearily.

Jennifer shrugged. "I guess a soda would be good. But I'm not letting you off the hook. I mean it, Zoe." She followed Zoe into the kitchen. "*Talk* to me." Her voice softened as she added, "please."

Zoe sighed. "I just couldn't handle it. I shouldn't have gone." Zoe handed Jennifer a can of soda, then opened her own can and took a sip.

"But you were doing so well," Jennifer protested. She frowned. "It was Ethan, wasn't it? When you found out he'd had cancer, you freaked out."

"Why didn't he tell me, Jennifer?" Zoe moaned. "Why did he have to keep it a secret?"

"Why does it matter? He's not sick now. You heard him. He's cured. Have you told him about all the times you were sick when you were a kid?"

"It's not the same, and you know it. All I ever had was flu and chicken pox. People *die* from cancer."

"People die from lots of things," Jennifer pointed out calmly.

"It's not the same," Zoe repeated.

Jennifer didn't say anything for a while. "No," she agreed at last, "I guess it isn't." She sighed. "Ethan's worried about you, you know. He said he tried to call you but your mother said you couldn't come to the phone. Why don't you call him?"

"I can't call him," Zoe mumbled. "I don't know what to say." Her eyes filled with tears.

Jennifer shook her head. "I hate to say this, Zoe, but I think you're acting like a real jerk. You should at least give Ethan a chance to explain. You're throwing away a great guy when you don't have to." She started walking toward the front of the house, and Zoe followed her.

"I wish it didn't scare me so much," Zoe said to Jennifer's back. "But it does, and I can't pretend it doesn't. I could try to act like the idea of cancer doesn't terrify me, but it would just be a matter of time before Ethan saw through it and then it would be over between us anyway. If it's going to end, it might as well end now."

Jennifer turned to face her. "He's leaving for Arizona tomorrow. You owe it to him to at least say good-bye. That might make you both feel better, and it would leave the door open for later. Once you get used to the idea that he's been sick, you might feel differently."

"I'll never feel differently," Zoe said softly.

Jennifer glared at her in frustration. "I only suspected it before, but now I know for sure. You have a cancer phobia, Zoe," she said. "And you'd better get over it now, before it messes up your life more than it already has!"

"How can I do that?" Zoe asked.

Jennifer took a deep breath. "One good way would be to spend at least a couple of hours every day for the rest of our vacation at the hospital with me." She added gently, "I know it won't be easy, but you've got to try."

Zoe shuddered. "I can't go back there again."

Jennifer snorted. "Can't—or won't?" She

grabbed her jacket off the rack, and yanked open the front door.

"How are you getting home?" Zoe asked as a blast of cold air rushed into the house.

"I'll walk," Jennifer almost yelled. "Hopefully, it'll cool me off!" She stepped outside and slammed the door.

Zoe leaned against the closed door for a minute, wiping the tears from her cheeks. *If only I hadn't agreed to go to the party,* she thought. *Maybe then I would never have found out the truth about Ethan, and we'd still be going out.*

But that never would have worked and Zoe knew it. Sooner or later, the truth would have come out. Sooner or later, she would have been forced to face the fact that Ethan had had cancer, and that one day she might lose him forever.

"Oh, Ethan," Zoe said aloud. She missed him so much. But loving someone with a life-threatening disease, even one that had supposedly been cured, was just too painful. Zoe had done that once before, and she still bore scars from the experience. Someone like Jennifer might be able to manage it, but Zoe knew she never could.

Chapter Ten

"What's bothering you, Zoe?" Minda asked as the girls left Kate's house together Wednesday morning after cheerleading practice. "You're not acting like yourself. Did you and Ethan have a fight or something?"

Zoe opened the door to Minda's car and got in. "Not really," Zoe answered.

"How did that thing at the hospital go? Okay? You did go, didn't you?"

Zoe sighed. "I went, all right."

"And it was as bad as you thought it would be," Minda guessed.

"Worse."

Minda started the car. Then she sat back and gave Zoe an appraising look. Zoe kept looking straight ahead while the engine idled.

When Minda finally put the car in gear and started driving, she said, "Look, if you don't want to talk about it, I understand."

"That's the trouble: I do want to talk about it, but I'm not sure I should," Zoe said.

"Suit yourself," Minda said. "It's entirely up to you. Only tell me if you want to."

It was too hard to keep everything all bottled up inside. "Okay," Zoe said. "I'll tell you, but you have to swear you won't tell a soul, not even Jeremy. It's about Ethan, and I'm pretty sure he doesn't want anyone to know about this."

Minda drew an imaginary *x* above her heart with one finger. "I swear I won't tell a soul. Not even Jeremy. What is it? Something awful? Has Ethan got a steady girlfriend in Arizona?"

"I'd almost be glad if that was it, but it isn't. It's much worse." Zoe paused to draw a deep breath before going on. "Ethan had cancer," she said. Just saying the word was difficult.

"*Cancer?*" Minda repeated. Her mouth fell open and she shook her head in disbelief. "Oh, Zoe!" she exclaimed. "That's *really* awful! When? He's not sick now, is he?"

"No. It was six or seven years ago, I guess," Zoe said. "Ethan told the kids at the hospital that he's cured. But cancer can come back." She stared out the window at the blanket of fresh snow covering everything, still stunned at how quickly her perfect life had fallen apart. First her father had gone. And now Ethan might go away, forever.

Minda's voice broke into her thoughts. "So what's the big secret if he's cured? Why doesn't he want anyone to know about it?" she asked. She turned up the Reilys' driveway and stopped the car.

Zoe shrugged. "Ethan told me he came here to get away from his parents. They were too overprotective. Maybe he's afraid that if other people find out, they'll treat him the same way."

"Why did he tell you about it, then?" Minda asked. "I guess he didn't know how you feel about that."

"He didn't really tell me," Zoe said. "I overheard him telling a group of kids about it at the hospital during the party."

Minda whistled. "And then what happened?"

Zoe cringed at the memory of the way she'd acted. She knew she'd done just what Ethan was probably afraid people would do if he told them about his illness. "When I heard that he'd had cancer, I was so upset I ran out of the party without saying anything to him, or to anyone," Zoe confessed. "Jennifer is furious with me, of course, and I don't blame her. I'm furious with myself. But I can't help the way I feel. I mean, I shouldn't pretend I'm something I'm not, should I?"

"Of course not," Minda agreed. "I probably would have done the same thing."

"Jennifer wouldn't have," Zoe said, biting the edge of her cuticle nervously. "Jennifer says I have a cancer phobia and I ought to be spending the rest of vacation working at the hospital with her so I can get over it."

Minda shuddered. "You're not thinking of following her advice, are you?"

"No," said Zoe. "I probably should, but I'm not strong enough to face those kids after letting them down the way I did. What I'm really thinking about is going to Australia to live with my dad. My sister's going right after New Year's, and I could go with her. That would make everything a whole lot easier, for both me and Ethan."

"Forget it!" Minda said vehemently. "There's got to be a better way."

"I can't think of one, and all I've done since Monday afternoon is think about this."

"Don't give up yet. I'll try to think of something, too," Minda said. "After all, if it weren't for me, you wouldn't be in this mess. I'm the one who made you meet Ethan."

"I'm not sorry I met him," Zoe murmured. 'It's the only thing I'm not sorry about!"

After Zoe got out of the car, she stood in the driveway a minute, watching Minda back out and pull away. When the car rounded the corner and was finally out of sight, Zoe went inside.

The house was quiet. Mrs. Reily was at work and Tara, Zoe remembered, was spending the day with a friend who lived on the other side of Edenvale.

Zoe hung her jacket up on the coatrack. Then she slowly climbed the stairs to her room. She wasn't sure that telling Minda about Ethan was the right thing to have done. She'd been giving more thought to how Ethan was feeling about the situation. Somehow, Zoe suspected, however bad she felt, Ethan probably felt worse.

When Zoe reached her room, she picked up her sketch pad from her desk. Drawing always made her feel better. It might also help her think more clearly.

After settling back on her bed, Zoe flipped open the cover of her sketch pad. Instead of the fresh sheet of paper she had expected, she saw the drawing she had made of Cindy at the party. Zoe realized that she had forgotten to give it to Cindy, and that made her feel awful. Then she remembered her promise to the other kids, the ones whose pictures she hadn't gotten to. She'd told Nina that her drawing would be next. Zoe could almost feel Nina's trusting hand nestled in hers, and suddenly she knew she had no choice. She had to go back to the hospital, no matter how hard it was for her. If she didn't, she would never be able to forgive herself.

Tossing her sketch pad aside, Zoe jumped off her bed. She felt surprisingly exhilarated. *Of course*, she told herself. *This is the answer, just as Jennifer had said.* Zoe would confront her fears head on by going to the hospital for at least part of every day from now until Ethan came back. If that didn't cure her phobia, at least she would have the satisfaction of knowing that she had tried. Maybe things could work out for her and Ethan after all.

Zoe hurried into the hall and quickly dialed Jennifer's number.

"She's at the hospital this morning," Mrs. Lund told her a minute later. "She told me she'd be home about four o'clock. Shall I have her call you, Zoe?"

"No. Thank you anyway, Mrs. Lund," Zoe said. "I'll see her before then. I'm going to the hospital myself."

As soon as Zoe had said good-bye and hung up, she picked up the phone again and dialed Minda's number.

"Hello?" Minda said.

"Oh, good! You're home!" Zoe cried happily.

"Zoe?" Minda said. "Is that you? You sound like a different person."

"I am," Zoe exclaimed. "At least I'm going to try and be a different person. I need to ask you a favor, though."

"Anything, as long as it isn't shopping for an Australian wardrobe," Minda joked.

"Can you give me a ride to Children's Hospital?"

"You're going back there?" Minda sounded surprised. "I thought you said you couldn't."

"I did, but I changed my mind. Can you take me?" Zoe pressed, eager to get going. She was afraid if she waited too long, she'd change her mind again or have second thoughts, and she knew she could afford neither.

"All right. If you're sure that's what you want," Minda said.

"It is! I'll explain everything in the car," Zoe promised.

"How soon will you be ready?"

"As soon as you get here." Then Zoe added, "Please hurry, Minda. I have to do this and if I wait too long, I might get cold feet."

"I'll be right there." Minda hung up without bothering to say good-bye.

Zoe hurried to get ready. Today, she decided, she would wear her gold cheerleading sweater and short white skirt. Maybe she'd even teach the kids a few cheers. But first she was going to finish those drawings, starting with Nina.

"You're wearing that to the hospital?" Minda asked incredulously when Zoe got into the car a few minutes later. "If I were you, I wouldn't worry about cold feet. It's your legs that are going to freeze."

Zoe laughed as she settled her sketch pad on the seat between Minda and herself. "It's part of my act," she said, fastening her seat belt.

Minda smiled. "Well, you sure look better."

"I am," Zoe said. She felt happier now than she had in days.

"So, what's going on?" Minda wanted to know.

"Drive," Zoe commanded, "and I'll explain."

As Minda drove, Zoe told her all about the winter-solstice party. She told her about Ethan's banjo playing and about the drawings the kids had asked Zoe to make for them. While they stopped at a traffic light, Zoe showed Minda her drawing of Cindy.

"She wants to be a glamorous model, a cover girl," Zoe explained.

"Who doesn't?" Minda quipped.

"She was wearing a scarf because all her hair fell out from her cancer treatments." The light turned green, and Zoe closed the sketch pad.

"That's sad," Minda said.

"That's the funny thing. I thought it would be *too* sad," Zoe said thoughtfully. "But it wasn't. There was something hopeful about it. All those kids are looking forward to growing up, to living normal lives. They haven't given up."

"Well, I think you're brave for going back again," Minda said.

Zoe shook her head. "I don't feel brave. Actually, I'm pretty scared. But I made some promises I didn't keep and I'm going to make up for it now."

Minda pulled up to the main doors of the hospital. "Good luck, and call me later. I want to know how it goes."

"Thanks, Minda." Zoe got out of the car, took a deep breath, and hurried inside.

"I'm looking for Jennifer Lund," she told the woman at the front desk. "She's a volunteer."

The woman smiled. "Is Jennifer a friend of yours?"

Zoe returned her smile. "Jennifer is one of my best friends," she replied.

"Then you're lucky," the woman said. "I think Jennifer's in the recreation room this morning. It's up on four."

"I know," Zoe said. "Thanks."

"Zoe!" Nina cried when Zoe came into the recreation room a few minutes later. The little girl ran over to her, all smiles.

"Zoe?" Jennifer said, looking up from the construction paper she'd been cutting, and staring at her friend. "What are you doing here?"

Zoe held up her sketchbook. "I have a job to finish," she said with a smile. She added hesitantly, "Is that okay?"

Jennifer beamed. "It's more than that! It's super! Coming here was definitely the right thing to do."

"I hope so," Zoe murmured.

"Draw me first, Zoe," Nina said. Throwing her arms around Zoe's waist, the little girl looked up at her. "Remember? You promised."

"I do remember, and that's why I'm here. A promise is a promise," Zoe told the child. "But first, I need to deliver this." Zoe opened the sketchbook and showed Jennifer and Nina the drawing of Cindy.

"I'll have to mail it," Jennifer said. "Cindy went home this morning."

"She's better?" Zoe asked hopefully. While Nina was admiring the drawing, Jennifer looked at Zoe and silently shook her head.

"Oh," was all Zoe could say. She felt the same dreadful feeling as when she'd heard Ethan talk about having cancer. But looking down at Nina, Zoe knew she couldn't run away this time. She couldn't do that to Nina again. She'd stick it out at least long enough to keep her promise.

"Well then, here," Zoe said. She tore the sketch out of her book and handed it to Jennifer. "Maybe you could take care of mailing this while Nina and I start our drawing."

Jennifer nodded and took the picture.

Taking Nina's hand in hers, Zoe led her to a table along the edge of the room. As soon as Zoe took off her jacket, Nina let out a squeal of delight.

"Are you a cheerleader, Zoe?" she asked. Zoe nodded. "Draw me in a cheerleading outfit just like yours!" Nina demanded.

"Okay," Zoe agreed. "Later, when I'm finished drawing, I can even teach you some cheers if you want me to."

"Really? That would be great!" Nina's eyes were shining. "I'm really glad you came back."

"So am I," Zoe said, and realized to her surprise that she really meant it.

Kids drifted in and out of the room as Zoe worked, and she found herself promising to do more sketches than she could possibly finish in a day. But that was all right, because Zoe knew now that she would be coming again. Her only wish was that Ethan could know what she was doing. Maybe he'd forgive her for running away when he realized how hard she was trying to overcome her fear.

"How about becoming a regular volunteer here?" Jennifer asked later that afternoon as she and Zoe were getting ready to go. "You'll get a great-looking outfit like mine," she teased.

"I kind of like this one," Zoe said, smoothing the fuzzy capital *E* on the front of her cheerleading sweater. "But thanks for the offer. I'll definitely think it over."

The girls made their way to the front of the building, stopping to say good-bye to several kids on their way.

"I'd like to help out here during vacation. I don't know about after that," Zoe said. "You know, I actually enjoyed myself today."

"You'd better be careful, Zoe," Jennifer warned. "You may find you're trading one problem for another."

Zoe frowned. "I don't understand."

"Instead of avoiding hospitals and sick people, you might find yourself seeking them out," Jennifer told her.

"You mean, like you?" Zoe teased.

Instead of answering, Jennifer said, "Well, here's Mom. Let's go. I don't know about you, but I'm beat."

"Are you coming back tomorrow?" Zoe asked as she followed Jennifer to the doors.

Jennifer nodded. "Some of the hospital staff will be taking Christmas Eve and Christmas off, but I kind of thought I'd come in both afternoons. Mom said she didn't mind. Some of the kids won't be having many visitors. I thought I could try to fill in the gaps and maybe make it a little less lonely for them." She pulled the door open and held it for Zoe.

"I'd like to come in with you," Zoe said. "Between the two of us, we could spread a lot of holiday cheer."

"Zoe, honey! The phone's for you," Mrs. Reily called from the foot of the stairs later that evening.

Zoe stuck her head into the hall. "Who is it?" she asked.

"A male," Mrs. Reily answered mysteriously.

Zoe's first thought was the caller was Ethan and her heart beat faster. She wasn't quite sure what she would say to him, but she was very glad he'd called. She could tell him about going back to the hospital. Zoe picked up the phone and carried it into her room.

"Hello?" she said eagerly once she was settled comfortably on her bed.

"Hi, honey. It's Dad."

"Dad!" Zoe was really surprised. Her mother had tricked her into talking to her father, but she was glad.

"I know it's early, but I wanted to wish you a Merry Christmas. It isn't always easy to get a line on a holiday."

"Oh, Dad," Zoe said, suddenly feeling like

she might cry. "I'm sorry I was so mad at you."

"Believe me, honey," her father said, "I understand. I hate making a promise I can't keep. But I did, and I'm sorry. I never meant to let you down."

"I know, Dad. I'm not mad anymore," Zoe assured him. "I understand. I mean, sometimes things happen that can't always be helped, right?"

"It sounds like you've done some growing up," her father observed.

"I hope so," Zoe said. Then they both laughed.

"My invitation still stands, you know," Mr. Reily went on. "I'd love to have you come here next week with your sister and finish out the school year."

"Sorry, Dad. I want to see you, but I can't leave Edenvale right now. I've got too many commitments right here."

"Are you talking about cheerleading? Or are you talking about a certain young man your mother and sister have been telling me about?" he teased.

"Hopefully, both," Zoe told him as an image of Ethan's smiling face flashed across her mind. "But maybe I can visit you this summer."

"I hope I'll be home by summer. But I'll be coming back here. Australia is a fantastic place, Zoe. I'd love to have all of you see it with me."

Zoe said, "I'd like that. I miss you, Dad."

"I miss you too, honey," he said. "I love you a lot."

"I love you too, Dad."

After she'd hung up, Zoe lay on her bed, staring up at the ceiling. She'd forgiven her father for letting her down and it hadn't been all that hard. Did she dare hope that Ethan would forgive her for letting him down, for getting scared and running away?

Chapter Eleven

Zoe was in her room getting ready to go to the hospital several days later when she heard the telephone ring in the upstairs hall. Before she could make a move to answer it, she heard Tara bolt out of her room yelling, "I've got it!"

Zoe picked up her brush and began to brush her hair. She'd only managed one stroke when Tara started pounding on her bedroom door.

"Phone, Zoe! It's a boy!" she yelled.

"Coming," Zoe called, trying to sound calmer than she felt. Every time the phone rang these days, Zoe hoped it was Ethan, although she knew he was still in Arizona.

Zoe was eager to talk to him now. She wanted to tell him why she'd acted the way she had, and that she was sorry for letting him down. But mostly, she just wanted to hear his voice.

"Hello," she said into the phone.

"Hello, Zoe," the deep, familiar voice replied. Hearing it nearly took Zoe's breath away. "It's Ethan. Ethan Anderson?" he added, as if Zoe might have forgotten him.

"Ethan!" Zoe exclaimed eagerly. "How are you? *Where* are you?"

"I'm fine," Ethan said. "I'm at Doug's. I came back a little early." He sounded guarded, as though he wasn't sure if Zoe would be pleased or not.

"When did you get here?" Zoe asked. She was starting to feel nervous. She was afraid she'd say something wrong.

"A couple of days ago. Look, I'm calling about the party," Ethan said, sounding a little impatient with their awkward conversation.

"Doug's party?" Zoe asked. Then, all at once, she was certain she knew why he'd called. Ethan wanted to break their date. *We're through*, she thought sadly. *And since everything is my fault, I should make it as easy for him as possible.*

"I was going to call you, you know, when you got back. I mean, I didn't know you were back yet," Zoe babbled, doing her best to sound cheerful. "Look, Ethan, something's come up. I'm afraid I can't go to the party after all."

"Oh," Ethan said. Zoe had expected him to sound relieved, but instead, his voice was neutral. That was even worse. "I see. Is Jennifer busy, too?"

"Jennifer?" Zoe echoed, surprised to hear Ethan mention her friend's name.

"We sort of made a deal with Jennifer, remember? She was going to go to Doug's party if we went . . ." His voice trailed off. "Anyway," Ethan began again, "I'll understand if she's changed her mind about going."

"I can't answer for Jennifer. Why don't you call her yourself?" Zoe was amazed at how breezy her voice sounded even though her heart felt as if it were breaking. Telling the boy she loved to call her best friend for a date certainly wasn't the easiest thing she'd ever done!

"Okay," Ethan said. There was a second of silence, then he added, "Well, I guess I'll be seeing you, then."

"Good-bye," Zoe said softly. She quickly hung up the phone before she started to cry.

"Ethan's back," was the first thing Zoe said to Jennifer when she got to the hospital later that day.

Jennifer looked up from the checkers game she'd been playing with Matthew. "I thought he wasn't coming back until tomorrow."

"He came back early," Zoe said. "He called me this morning."

"King me!" Matthew ordered Jennifer. He looked up at Zoe and grinned. "Jennifer is even worse at checkers than you are, Zoe."

Zoe returned Matthew's smile. Volunteering at the hospital hadn't saved her relationship with Ethan, but she didn't regret the time she'd spent with Matthew and Nina and the other kids. She felt she'd made at least a small difference in their lives, and a great difference in her own.

"Maybe you've just gotten better since the last time we played, Matthew. Ever think of that?" Zoe said.

"Maybe," Matthew agreed modestly. "I guess I'll have to play you again to find out. How about it?"

"It's a deal," Zoe said, giving the visor of his baseball cap a gentle tug.

While Zoe and Matthew were talking, Jennifer stared intently at the board. Finally she covered Matthew's red checker with another one. Then she slid one of her black checkers forward. Matthew shook his head.

"Are you sure you want to do that, Jennifer?" he asked. He sounded more like one of the teachers at the high school than a nine-year-old boy.

"Positive," Jennifer said confidently. She lifted the finger she'd been keeping on the checker while she decided, and Matthew quickly triple-jumped her, ending the game.

"I win again!" Matthew shouted triumphantly. He clasped his hands together and waved his thin arms over his head. "Hail to the champ!"

Jennifer pretended to scowl at him. "I need a break, Matthew," she said. "You've tied my poor brain into knots with all your advanced checker strategy." She got up and motioned for Zoe to follow her.

"Okay. Zoe and I will play now," Matthew said, his face breaking out into a big grin.

"Sorry, Matthew. I'm taking Zoe with me."

Matthew shrugged. "Okay. Maybe Rick will play with me." The motor on Matthew's wheelchair whirred as he rolled away.

"I think it's time to teach that kid chess,"

Jennifer said, holding the recreation room door open for Zoe. She added, "Why don't you sound happier about hearing from Ethan? I would have thought you'd be thrilled that he's back and that he called you." The girls started walking down the corridor toward the solarium, where several vending machines were located.

"I don't know what I expected," Zoe said sadly, "but it wasn't what I got. He only called me to cancel our date for New Year's Eve. I think he wants to take you to Doug's party now."

"Me? I thought the three of us were going together," Jennifer said. She slipped some quarters into the soda machine. When a cola came rolling down the chute, Jennifer picked up the can and handed it to Zoe.

"Thanks," Zoe said. She popped the tab but didn't drink any of the soda. "I knew he wanted to break our date, so before he could say anything, I told him I'd made other plans. But he still wants you to go with him. He'll probably call you tonight." Before she could catch herself, a tear rolled down Zoe's face. She dashed it off, before Jennifer turned around.

Jennifer put several more quarters into the machine and pushed the cola button again.

When the can rolled out, she picked it up and popped it open.

"I guess I don't get it," Jennifer said after taking a sip. "Why did you say you couldn't go?"

"I've decided to spend New Year's Eve here with the kids. I've been thinking about it for a while, and today, while I was talking to Ethan, I finally made up my mind." Zoe forced herself to smile. "Really, Jennifer, it's what I want."

Jennifer shook her head. "I guess you think you're doing something brave and noble here, but you're really running away again. I hope you know that."

"I am not!" Zoe insisted. "I'm sure the only reason Ethan called me this morning was to break our date, so I made it easy for him by breaking it first. He was the one who mentioned your name. I just made sure he knew it was all right with me if he called you."

"Now I know you're nuts," Jennifer said, shaking her head. "Why would I want to go out with your boyfriend? I suppose you don't think I'm capable of finding a boyfriend on my own?"

"That's not it and you know it! Anyway, Ethan isn't my boyfriend," Zoe said. "We only met a few weeks ago. Things didn't work out for us, that's all. It's no big deal." Zoe didn't really believe it and she could tell Jennifer didn't believe it, either.

"So what exactly do you want me to do?" Jennifer asked.

Zoe said quietly, "I want you to do whatever you want to do. If you want to go to Doug's party with Ethan, go. I mean, don't not go because of me, okay?"

Jennifer scowled at Zoe but all she said was, "Okay."

Chapter Twelve

"Look out, everyone," Zoe cried, pushing the silly paper hat she'd been wearing farther back on her head. She shook the big silver firecracker in her hand. "I don't know what this thing is going to do, and I don't want anybody getting hurt when it explodes."

"Light it!" Matthew urged, rolling in a little closer to get a better look.

Zoe set the cracker down and put a match to the long fuse. As it started to sizzle, Zoe said, "Get back, everyone! It's going to go!"

All at once the large silver cracker made a disappointingly puny sort of popping sound. But then the cardboard lid flew off and out sailed streamers, confetti, whistles, and dozens of brightly colored paper hats. The kids who were well enough to come into the recreation room that evening all laughed and clapped their hands.

"Light another one," Nina pleaded, tugging on Zoe's arm.

"Later," Zoe promised. "Now we're going to watch that movie Rick rented for you guys, the one about an abominable snowman who moves in with a regular family."

"It's great," Matthew assured Nina. "I've seen it three times already, so I know."

Zoe helped everyone get comfortable while Rick and another volunteer set up the big-screen TV and VCR. Zoe handed out small bags of popcorn they'd made earlier. She had just turned out the lights when she felt a hand on her shoulder.

She turned around, expecting to see one of the attendants or perhaps a nurse. Instead, she saw Ethan.

"Ethan!" Zoe gasped. "What are you doing here? Why aren't you at Doug's party?"

"It wasn't much fun without you," he said softly.

Zoe peered over his shoulder. Her heart was pounding so loudly she was afraid he could hear it. "Where's Jennifer?"

"She's still at the party. The last time I saw

her, she was dancing with Doug." Ethan grinned. "Doug's going to have to watch himself. Jennifer will be dancing circles around him in no time."

Zoe smiled tremulously. "I know just what you mean. Jennifer can be a real steamroller when she has her mind set on something."

"You can say that again," Ethan agreed with a sigh.

"Do you mean that she steamrolled you?" Zoe asked, jealousy and regret making her voice shake slightly.

"Let's just say you're lucky to have her for a friend. She told me that you and I are more alike than either of us wanted to admit. She said we both have problems and instead of dealing with them, we run away."

Puzzled, Zoe said, "Both of us? I know what she means about me, but not about you."

"Shhh!" one of the kids near them hissed. "I can't hear the movie!"

Ethan took Zoe's hand. "Let's go somewhere else. We need to talk, and we're disturbing the kids."

"All right." Zoe let Ethan lead her out of the recreation room. "There's a couch in the solarium by the vending machines," she told him.

When they reached the solarium, they sat at opposite ends of the couch, facing each other. Zoe couldn't figure out what was going on. Why wasn't Ethan at the party with Jennifer? That was where he wanted to be—and who he wanted to be with—wasn't it?

"So," Zoe said after they'd sat in silence for a few seconds: "What are you really doing here, Ethan?"

"Isn't that obvious?"

Zoe shook her head. "Not to me."

"Jennifer tried to make me come here the minute I arrived at her house to pick her up, but I wouldn't do it," Ethan told her. "But once we were at the party, I realized she was right. I had to see you, and I had to see you tonight. This thing between us has gone on long enough."

"I didn't think you wanted to see me again after I ran out on you at the children's party," Zoe whispered, lowering her gaze.

"And I didn't think *you* wanted to see *me*. Jennifer told me how you felt about cancer, Zoe. I know I should have told you about it before, but I didn't know how to go about it," Ethan confessed. "At first, I wasn't going to tell you at all. You see, when I came to Edenvale, I just wanted to be treated like a normal person. As far as I was concerned, the cancer was just something that happened, like any other illness that's over. Do you understand? It was so important for so long. Once it was gone, once the doctors said I was cured, I just wanted to pretend it had never happened. Here in Edenvale, nobody knew I'd been sick except my aunt and uncle and Doug. They've been much cooler about the whole thing than my own family could be. But then, they didn't see me when I was at my worst. My parents did."

"I understand," Zoe said softly. "My aunt had cancer, but she didn't get better. Ever since she died, I've avoided hospitals and sick people. Jennifer must have asked me a million times to come here with her, and I'd always turned her down. It wasn't very honest of me not to tell you about that, either. I was afraid you'd think less of me if I did."

Ethan reached across the space between them and took Zoe's hand. "If you'd told me that, I might have kept my secret longer."

"I thought of that. But I would have found out sometime, and everything that's happened would have happened anyway," Zoe said. 'Only it might have been even worse if it had happened later."

"I'm not sorry that it's all out in the open, that's for sure. It was harder keeping it to myself than I thought it was going to be," Ethan admitted. "Doug was the only person at Edenvale High I really felt comfortable with. Until I met you, that is."

"And then I let you down," Zoe murmured.

Ethan shook his head. "No, you didn't. Jennifer told me about how you've thrown yourself into volunteering ever since the party. I'm proud of you, Zoe. I really mean it."

Zoe blushed. "Helping out here has forced me to deal with some of my fears," she said. "I think I understand now about that second kind of perfect you described, even though I still can't be very happy about it."

"Then there's still a chance for us?" Ethan's dark brown eyes were glowing. "Do you want that as much as I do?"

"Oh, yes," Zoe cried, catching hold of both his hands and holding onto them tightly. "I can't think of anything I want more!"

"I care about you, Zoe Reily. I really do. From now on I'll be honest with you no matter how scared I am. I want to trust you, and I want you to trust me."

"Oh, Ethan," Zoe whispered. "I've missed you so much!"

Taking hold of her shoulders, Ethan drew her close. "I'm back now," he murmured. Then he covered her lips with his.

166

"All right, you two, break it up!"

Startled, Zoe pulled away. Rick and another volunteer were standing by the soda machine.

"It's not New Year's yet," Rick teased, giving them a playful wink. "No kissing allowed until midnight."

Ethan gave Rick a radiant grin. "It's got to be midnight somewhere in the world," he pointed out as the two volunteers left with their sodas. He drew Zoe close for another kiss.

STARFIRE

Romance Has Never Been So Much Fun!

☐ **IN SUMMER LIGHT**
By Zibby Oneal   25940-7 $2.95
The last place on earth Kate wants to spend the summer is at home with her parents. Kate can't escape the overpowering presence of her father, a famous artist who insists on ruling everybody's life, including her own. Then graduate student Ian Jackson arrives, and much to Kate's surprise the handsome young man helps Kate learn about herself and see her father in a new light.

☐ **CAMP GIRL-MEETS-BOY**
By Caroline B. Cooney   27273-X $2.95
Welcome to Camp Menunkechogue! For Marissa, finally a counselor, camp is what she lives for. For Vi, camp is a place to meet and catch a boyfriend. Grab your gear and join them for camp songs, romance, and great summer friendships!

☐ **CAMP REUNION**
By Caroline B. Cooney   27551-8 $2.95
Everyone's invited to Camp Men for a weekend reunion. Tans have faded but not the memories as Vi and Marissa meet up with their summer loves. Will it work out this time around?

STARFIRE

Books *you'll* want to read...and keep

☐ HOME SWEET HOME
by Jeanne Betancourt
16-year-old Tracy Jensen is not looking forward to leaving New York City to move with her family to her grandmother's farm. Tracy feels isolated at first, but when she meets Russian exchange student Ariya and gets involved in the town's activities she sees that life on the land offers many more rewards than she'd ever anticipated. 27857-6 $2.95/$3.50 in Canada

☐ THE SILVER GLOVE
by Suzie McKee Charnas
Heroine of *The Bronze King*, 14-year-old Valentine Marsh must help her remarkable, magical grandmother fight a powerful wizard who's come to Earth to steal human souls—and is masquerading as Val's new school psychologist! *The Silver Glove* is full of suspense, chilling chase scenes, magic & love. 27853-3 $2.95/$3.50 in Canada

☐ CAUGHT IN THE ACT: ORPHAN TRAIN QUARTET, BOOK 2 by Joan Lowery Nixon
In the second novel of THE ORPHAN TRAIN QUARTET, 11-year-old, Mike fears that he will be sent back to New York City to serve his prison sentence as a convicted thief. But the German family which has adopted him seems to be involved in much worse than stealing—murder! Mike vows to uncover the truth, even if his own life is in danger.
27912-2 $2.95/$3.50 in Canada

☐ THE GIRL WHO INVENTED ROMANCE
by Caroline B. Cooney, author of 'Among Friends'
As she watches her friends and family playing at romance, 16-year-old Kelly Williams has a great idea— she'll create a board game that sets down the rules of the romance game. It's easy for Kelly to see how others should act, but it's much more difficult when it comes to her own feelings for Will! (A Starfire Hardcover).
05473-2 $13.95/$15.95 in Canada